Life Ain't Over Yet

by

Lee Heide

Cover—'The Old Sailor', Sidney, B.C.

Printed in Victoria, Canada.

Note for Librarians: a cataloguing record for this book that includes Dewey Classification and US Library of Congress numbers is available from the National Library of Canada. The complete cataloguing record can be obtained from the National Library's online database at:
www.nlc-bnc.ca/amicus/index-e.html
ISBN 1-4120-2282-7

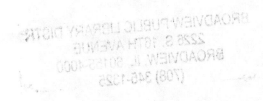

This book was published on-demand in cooperation with Trafford Publishing.
On-demand publishing is a unique process and service of making a book available for retail sale to the public taking advantage of on-demand manufacturing and Internet marketing. On-demand publishing includes promotions, retail sales, manufacturing, order fulfilment, accounting and collecting royalties on behalf of the author.
Suite 6E, 2333 Government St., Victoria, B.C. V8T 4P4, CANADA
Phone   250-383-6864   Toll-free   1-888-232-4444 (Canada & US)
Fax   250-383-6804   E-mail   sales@trafford.com
Web site www.trafford.com   TRAFFORD PUBLISHING IS A DIVISION OF TRAFFORD HOLDINGS LTD.
Trafford Catalogue #04-0110   www.trafford.com/robots/04-0110.html
10   9   8   7   6   5   4   3   2

Contents

Life Ain't Over Yet

George Dixon slammed down the piano lid in disgust and marched over to the bar where he poured himself a stiff rye with a touch of water.

His wife, Anne, looked up from her book. 'Not going well?'

'Not going at all,' he growled, running a hand through his abundant grey hair.

'Wearing a track to the bar won't help,' she said, tartly, taking off her glasses.

George took a healthy swallow but didn't reply.

'Anyhow,' she continued 'you don't have a deadline, do you?'

'No,' he admitted. 'Muriel wants to put the play on in the winter... it's only May now.'

'I haven't read the script. How many songs do you have to write?'

'Five or six. All to do with Seniors—it's a sort of geriatric musical comedy.'

'Well,' Ann observed brightly, 'you're the right age... 68 years old.'

'Yeah, but I think I'm getting senile. Can't write my music, can't play golf decently any more...' He went back to the bar. 'Do you want a drink?'

'A sherry, please. Let's sit on the front deck.' She led the way outside to a spectacular view of Lake Okanagan. 'We sure did the right thing, coming to Kelowna to retire,' she said, settling into a deck chair with a contented sigh.

'Well, neither of us could stand the winters in Winnipeg any longer.'

'And prices were so good four years ago.' Ann paused. 'We can afford to live decently now that the house is paid for.'

George sighed. 'Sometimes I think I should have been a musician instead of an insurance agent. Might have made a million dollars with some hit songs.'

1

'And we might have starved to death, too. Oh, I don't mean that you don't have the talent,' she added quickly, 'but you had to start earning a living at once after the war. Circumstances alter cases and one has to do the best one can at any given time.'

'You're becoming quite a philosopher.' George looked at her fondly; she was still pretty with her peaches-and-cream complexion and white hair, although she moved rather slowly now.

'Old age and philosophy travel together.'

'Right.'

'Are you playing golf tomorrow?' she asked.

George looked dejected. 'I guess so.'

'What's the matter? You usually can't wait to get on the course.'

'I dunno. I'm not playing well.' He stood up. 'Do you want another sherry?'

'No, thanks.'

'I'll have one.' He went inside.

Ann sighed. His increased drinking was becoming worrisome.

'Are you the oldest in your foursome?' she asked, when he returned.

'Yes. The other three are still working.' George snorted. 'A doctor, a lawyer and a priest! How did I get stuck with three such stuffed shirts?'

'They're not...' Ann started.

'Three balloons of pomposity... fat and full of hot air... hanging about...'

'Which you just love to prick!' Ann Dixon knew her husband well.

'You bet!'

'Just don't puncture them too often or you'll be playing alone!'

'It's okay,' George took a healthy swallow. 'Half of the time they don't realize they're being shafted.'

'I wonder,' Ann mused. Noticing that his drink was nearly empty and wishing to forestall him getting another, she said: 'Let's go for a walk down by the water.'

George stood up. 'Okay... I'll try to find enough energy.'

'Why are you so tired?'

'Oh, who knows? I don't have the stamina for anything any more.

If I'm playing golf in the afternoon, I can't work in the garden in the morning—I'd be too tired. If we're going out in the evening, I have to take it easy all day, or I might fall asleep on my host. Before I went to bed last night I rubbed some *535* on my bad leg, put some *Preparation H* on my pile, and a corn plaster on my toe. I'm falling apart! GOLDEN YEARS! BULLSHIT!'

'Go and see Hubert Bauer,' she said, sharply. 'You've got a doctor in your foursome—make use of him.'

'I'm not so sure that Kraut knows what he is doing.'

'You shouldn't call him that!'

'I fought the Germans for five years and that entitles me to call them Krauts if I want to.'

'Well... maybe... but not to his face. You know how sad he's been since his wife died.'

'Yeah... okay. He's got a sense of humour like the Brandenburg Gates.'

'Anyhow,' Ann continued, vehemently, 'you haven't been for a check-up in years. It's ridiculous! At our age, we should have one every year.'

'Well, I...'

'You have to go! You may have something seriously wrong. Who knows what...'

'All right... all right,' George gave in. 'I'll go.'

George Dixon miraculously found a parking place on Bernard Ave., right in front of Dr. Bauer's office. But it didn't improve his mood much; next to dentists, doctors were a second on his hate list. After fifteen minutes in an austere waiting room, he was allowed in to the inner sanctum.

'Come in, George,' Hubert boomed. 'Have a seat.' Bauer's Germanic heritage was evident. He was a large, fleshy man, his head set on wide shoulders with no apparent neck, and small eyes. 'Now, what seems to be the trouble?'

George sat down. 'I'm tired all the time... no energy at all.'

'Were you very tired after our golf game on Saturday?'

'Yes,' George replied, abruptly, 'and I played like a drub.'

'Yes... well,' Hubert looked down at the empty form on his desk and adjusted his glasses. 'Who was your last doctor?'

'Don't have one.'

Hubert was startled. 'You've been in Kelowna for four years and not gone to a doctor?'

'Nope.'

'In that case, we'd better have a good check-up. Strip down to your shorts.'

On the scale, Bauer measured Dixon's height and weight. 'H...m...m... 185 lbs... you're about ten pounds over-weight for your height.'

'Yeah,' George said. 'I know.'

Bauer continued to probe, tap and listen for the best part of twenty minutes, filling in a medical form as he went.

'Well,' George remarked, 'you're sure thorough, you Kr... ah... you doctors. Where did you go to medical school—in Germany?'

Bauer was startled. 'Of course not! I was seven years old when my parents came to Vancouver. I went to U.B.C.'

'Oh, yeah... right... that's where you met Marion, wasn't it?'

'Yes.'

'Too bad that she's gone,' George sympathized.

Hubert sighed. 'Yes... I miss her.' He took off his glasses and rubbed the bridge of his nose. 'I was going to retire soon—I'm 62 years old—and we were going to do some travelling. But now...'

'And you don't have any children, do you?' Not waiting for an answer, 'Yeah, you might as well keep on working. Can I get dressed now?'

'Yes.'

'What's the verdict?' George asked, as he put his clothes back on.

'What?' Bauer asked. He was hard of hearing but would not admit it.

'I said: What's the matter with me?' George raised his voice.

'There's some stiffness in your right leg,' Bauer commenced. 'Does it bother you?'

'When it's damp; I picked up some shrapnel during the war. A Kr... ah... a German shell.'

'There's not much we can do about it. If it gets worse we can try electronic wave penetration. A more serious problem is your hypertension.'

'What's that?'

'High blood pressure.'

'Why can't you say so? Is it bad?'

'It isn't a disease in itself,' Hubert lectured, 'but it is indicative of trouble elsewhere.'

'My dad had it. My mother used to make him watermelon tea.'

'Watermelon seeds do contain a chemical that dilates the blood vessels. However, hypertension is not hereditary.'

'So what's causing it?'

'I don't know yet,' Bauer admitted.

'Oh, great!' George gave his sardonic smile. 'I'll rush home and plant some watermelons.'

'There are some things we can do. Hospital tests will show if you have a kidney complaint. If the principal artery to one kidney is narrowed and doesn't bring a sufficient supply of blood, the kidney secretes a hormone into the blood stream that causes high blood pressure. Surgery can correct that.'

'I don't like the sound of that,' George said.

'Don't worry too much. I don't think that is the cause. We can alleviate the high pressure in other ways.'

'Like what?'

'Avoid salty foods such as bacon, cheese, and canned goods. I'll give you a diet sheet. And I'll give you a prescription for a drug called *Reserpine* and for some vitamins that will help your energy level.'

'Is that all?'

'No. You need to remain more calm... not get agitated... reduce strain... take a more philosophical view of life.'

'Yeah,' George said, skeptically.

'Also,' Bauer continued, 'how much are you drinking?'

George paused. 'Not a lot.'

'Be specific,' Bauer ordered. 'Three drinks a day... five... seven?'

'I'd say about four.'

'Too many! You'll have to cut that down.'

'To what?'

'One drink a day.'

'Bloody Hell!' George exploded. 'What're you trying to do—take all the pleasure out of life?'

'I'm trying to get you healthy.'

'Why? So I can live to be 80 instead of 75? Who cares?'

'Why did you come to me?' Hubert demanded, 'if you're not prepared to follow my advice?'

'Ann pushed me into it,' George mumbled.

'What's that?' Bauer held his hand to his ear.

'Ann wanted me to,' George shouted.

'She only has your best interests at heart,' Bauer said, soothingly. 'After all, she is reaching the age where she shouldn't have any extra strain either. She has her own health to worry about.'

'Yeah,' George admitted, 'I guess so.'

Hubert stood up. 'Here is your diet sheet. I'll let you know when the hospital tests are scheduled.'

George accepted the sheet. 'I'll go along with that.' But as he left the office he mumbled: 'One drink a day…' He shook his head.

When George returned home in the late afternoon, Ann was reading a letter from their son, Michael, who lived in Winnipeg. She put it down at once to ask: 'What did Dr. Bauer have to say?'

'Well, he poked and pummelled and jotted everything down with a stone face.'

'Do you have to have an E.C.G.?'

'Nope.'

'Well,' she said, impatiently, 'he must have found something.'

'Yeah. I'm ten pounds over-weight and I have high blood pressure.'

'How high?'

'Oh, I don't know the numbers.'

'What do you have to do for it?'

'He gave me a prescription and a list of stuff that I can't eat.' George handed her the diet sheet. 'Everything I like most is on it.'

'I'll see to that,' she said, forcefully, scanning the forbidden list. 'Anything else?'

'I have to be calm and peaceful… reduced strain… not get excited.'

Ann gave a meager smile. 'Did he say anything about drinking?'

'Mine or his?'

'Yours, of course.'

'His patients only have a problem if they drink more than he does,' George replied, neatly avoiding the question. 'And since the sun's over the yardarm...' He headed for the bar. Changing the subject, he asked: 'Who is the letter from?'

'Michael.'

'Anything new?'

'Not a great deal. Jeffrey had a six-month birthday party.' She sighed. 'I wish we lived closer to them.'

'Yeah,' George commiserated. 'How about we go back for Xmas this year?'

'Oh!' Ann brightened. 'That would be great. Michael says that we could live there in a Granny Flat.'

'A Granny Flat! What the hell is that?'

'It's a portable home like a trailer only bigger and better... he could put it up in his back yard... we would be on our own but could visit them in the house whenever we wanted to... if we were sick or anything.'

'Ha!' George exclaimed. 'If you think I'm going to live in some dog kennel in his back yard through a Manitoba winter, forget it!'

'You're probably right,' Ann said. 'By the way, did you change your Will to add Jeffrey?'

'No, not yet.'

'Well, you should.'

'Yeah. I'll speak to Walter Branscombe when we play golf on Saturday.'

On Monday afternoon, George Dixon drove the short distance to the lawyer's office in Capri Centre. It was a hot day and he wore a sports shirt and slacks. After a short wait, he was ushered into the inner office.

'Hello, George,' Walter greeted, 'it's rather a warm day, isn't it?'

'Sure is,' George agreed, wondering how Walter knew; the office was air conditioned and he wore a dark suit with a white shirt and a Navy tie. 'Look—tell that girl of yours that old people aren't automatically cretins.'

'What do you mean?'

'Every time she sees my grey hair she starts to use words of one syllable and a patient tone of voice that implies I may not even then understand.'

'Oh, I'm sure she's only being polite, old boy.' Branscombe had spent the war years in the Canadian Navy and the de *riguer* British expressions were still with him.

'Patronizing ain't politeness.'

'I'll mention it to her,' Walter said. 'By the way, you still owe me five dollars for golf—we didn't have any change.'

'Yeah.' George fished a five-dollar bill from his pocket. 'Hope you choke on it.'

'How come your golf is so poor these days?'

'I dunno,' George replied. 'Hubert's given me some pills—maybe they'll spruce me up.'

'I hope so. Actually,' Walter continued, 'I'm glad you came in. There is something I want to ask you.'

'What?' George asked, warily.

'I'm thinking of running for alderman in the next civic election and I badly need some help with my campaign.'

'Aren't you a bit long in the tooth to be entering politics?'

'Well—I'm 63 years old but… It's not so much that I want to be in politics, it's just that I feel I'm not well enough known in the city.'

'For a Judgeship?' George asked, shrewdly.

Walter started; he hadn't realized that George was so perceptive. 'Well—should it arise…'

'I'll think about it,' George said. He thought that Walter would make a good candidate; he was tall and handsome, looked younger than his years in spite of some loss of hair and had a smooth, urbane manner.

'Good! That's all I ask.' Walter stood up. 'Excuse me for a moment; I have to pay a visit.' He opened a door to reveal a small washroom and went in.

George had noticed before that Walter had weak kidneys and often had to go into the bushes when on the golf course. When he returned, George remarked: 'Pretty fancy!'

'Yes,' Branscombe agreed. 'When I had it put in, the plumber gave me a horrible bill.' 'Ye Gods,' I said, 'even I can't charge prices like that!"

'And…?'

"Neither could I,' he said, 'when I was practicing law."

George laughed. 'I don't believe that.' He looked around the office. 'I don't suppose you've got a bar, as well?'

'No,' Walter frowned. 'We don't seem to be getting around to the reason for your visit.' He shuffled some papers on his desk and donned a pair of granny glasses. 'Now, let's see… you have two children?'

'Yes. A boy and a girl. We decided that one was not enough and discovered that two was far too many.'

'And now a grandchild, born to Michael's wife.'

'Yeah—Karen isn't married. Not that that precludes having a child these days.'

'What do you want to do? Have him inherit if Michael dies?'

'Yes—in trust until he's old enough. And a lump sum when he's twenty-one.'

'How much?' asked Walter.

'Let's say $25,000.'

'All right. What is the boy's name?'

'Jeffrey Robert.'

'Right.' Walter made a note. 'A codicil to your Will should be sufficient.'

'What's a codicil?'

'An addition.'

'Then why don't you say so… you lawyers…' George paused. 'What's your charge for this codicil?'

'Our standard fee is $100.'

'$100!' George exploded. 'Just for adding a paragraph to my Will?'

'It's a set rate.'

'You're not dealing with one of your big corporations now,' George said, sternly, 'I'm just an old age pensioner.'

'Yes, but…'

'Hell—you'll dictate it to you secretary in two minutes!'

'There is more than…'

'In fact,' George interrupted again, 'she probably does the whole thing.'

'Well,' Walter weakened, 'how about a ten percent reduction since you're a friend?'

'Balls! Young Hunter down the street is drawing up a whole Will for $50.'

'He doesn't have our overhead.'

'You mean, your fancy bathroom. That's your problem—not mine.'

Walter sighed. 'What would you consider a fair price?'

'$50.'

'Not possible,' Walter said, firmly. '$75—and then I'll have trouble with our accountant.'

'Okay—$75 it is.' George smiled at the lawyer's discomfort. 'Don't take it to heart—WALT-ER.'

Branscombe sighed. 'Every peasant has a lawyer inside of him.'

Ann Dixon's bridge club met on Tuesday afternoons. Returning home, she was delighted to hear the sounds of the piano. 'Oh, good!' she thought, 'George is back at his music again.' Entering the living room, she saw him seated at the piano with paper strewn around; and a drink on the lid. 'How is it going?' she greeted.

George looked up. 'Only fair. I still can't get any musical inspiration, so I'm stealing at the moment.'

'Stealing what?'

'Listen,' he ordered, playing. 'Recognize the tune?'

Ann hummed a few bars. 'Sure… it's Rosemary Clooney's song—'This Ole House."

'Right! I'm thinking of using it for the opening song in the play. The leading lady is about your age, 66, and is lamenting her aches and pains, so I've written new words.'

George began to play and sing:

THIS OLE BODY

This ole body's had its battles,
This ole body's had its strife,
This ole body's had its torments
As I fought the storm of life.

This ole body's done its duty,
This ole body's served me well,
But it trembles in the darkness
As I hear the judgement bell.

CHORUS

Ain't gonna need this body no longer,
Ain't gonna need this head no more.
I forget to take my pills,
I forget to wash the floor,
I forget to feed the dog
Or to clean the window pane,
Ain't gonna need this body no longer,
I'm gettin' ready to meet the Saint.

My ole heart has had a bypass,
My ole blood has up and died,
And I've lost so many organs
That there's nothin' left inside.

My ole muscles are tired and flabby,
My ole bones are apt to crack,
My ole joints all have arthritis
And a disc's gone in my back.

-CHORUS-

My ole ears have lost their hearin',
My ole mouth has lost its spit,

I can eat a steak no longer
With these dentures that don't fit.

My ole feet are flat and corny,
My ole ankles swell in heat,
And I hold up all the traffic
When I try to cross the street.

-CHORUS-

'That's great!' Ann enthused. 'She feels just like I did last night.'

'I heard you prowling around in the night. What was the trouble?'

'My arthritis was acting up. Aches and pains are always worse at night.'

'Yeah… it's tough. You know what the bookmaker said?'

'No.'

'All of life is six-to-five against.'

'Yes. By the way, how did you make out with Walter?'

'Eckually, old bean,' George put on an exaggerated English accent, 'it went rahther well. Nipped him down a bit, doncha know.'

'What do you mean?'

'He wanted $100 for the job but I got him down to $75.' He went to the bar for a fresh drink.

'How did you do that?'

'By pleading poverty and by saying that young Hunter was doing whole Wills for $50.'

'How do you know that?'

'I don't… but Walter doesn't know that.'

'Oh, you liar,' Ann laughed. 'What did you put in your Will for Jeffrey?'

'$25,000 when he reaches 21 years old.'

'He will find that useful.'

'I made it 21 because by then he'll be able to do as he likes without parental interference. Blow it all if he wants to. Like the guy who ran through a million dollar inheritance in two years. When asked how he had done it, he replied: 'Well—I spent a lot on drinks and gambling and there were quite a few women. I guess I spent the rest foolishly."

'Did you tell that story to Walter?'

'No, but I will.' He paused. 'There's some mail on the hall table…
a letter from Karen.'

'Oh, good!' Ann rose stiffly and went to pick up the letters, immediately opening the one from their daughter. After a moment
she began to chuckle.

'What's funny?' George asked.

'She's still working for the advertising agency but now she's doing commercials for kids' TV. She says: 'They believe everything
they see on TV. Father is a moron, mother is a gossip, all old people
are either arthritic or constipated and spend all their time by the
telephone waiting for a long distance call'!'

'Right on! Has she got a new boy friend yet?'

'Yes… he's from Korea.'

'God!' George exclaimed. 'I hope we don't have any coffee-
coloured grandkids.'

'Oh, you always assume the worst.'

'I'm just being realistic. Do you think they're not sleeping together?'

'Well…'

'Of course they are… I just hope they're careful.' He proceeded
to the bar.

'How many drinks have you had today?' Ann asked, sharply.

'Oh… a couple.'

'Your 'couple' is the world's most flexible number.'

'It doesn't do any harm.'

'It does so,' she responded, hotly. 'Remember the time you came
home drunk and ran the car into the side of the garage?'

'Good Lord! That was thirty years ago!'

'It doesn't matter. Any time now, you'll do the same thing again.'
Ann marched out of the room, her back straight and her head high.

Father James Preston was not an ordinary Roman Catholic priest.
Raised in Calgary of religious parents, he was about to enter theo-
logical college, at age 19, when World War Two erupted. As a con-
scientious objector, he was exempt from military service but joined

the Red Cross as an ambulance driver, serving under fire in Italy. Returning home in 1946, he found that he was restless and not ready to enter the priesthood. Instead, he joined the Merchant Marine and roamed the world for 13 years. Finally, he came back to Calgary, entered the seminary, and was ordained at the age of 42 years. His travels and experiences had made him liberal and open-minded; together with his natural empathy for people and his gentle disposition, he was a favourite with all his parishioners.

His church office was simply furnished with a desk, a few chairs, and a large cross on the wall. He rose as Ann Dixon entered. 'I'm so glad you could find the time to come in today,' he smiled. His face was lined and weather-beaten from his years at sea. 'Do sit down.'

Ann smiled wryly as she took a chair. 'Time is not a scarce commodity when one is retired.'

'I suppose not.'

'You'll find out.' She paused. 'I guess priests do retire?'

'Oh, yes.' Preston gave a small, sweet smile. 'The days are gone when we were expected to die in harness, dropping in the middle of the *Gloria*. But I hope to soldier on until I'm seventy—another six years.'

'Will they keep you in this Parish, Father?'

'This will be my last posting. I'm too old for a promotion now and I really don't want one. I'm happy in a Parish and probably wouldn't be anywhere else.' He paused. 'But I'm sure you didn't ask to see me to discuss my retirement.'

'Ah… no.' Ann hesitated. 'I wanted to talk to you about George.'

'Yes…' he encouraged.

'Have you noticed that he is drinking a lot more lately?'

'Yes, I have. We used to have just one drink after golf but now he has three or four. And his golf game is poor, too. Do you know the reason?'

'I think so. He's worried about old age. He sees himself falling apart physically and losing the ability to compete. He's always been very competitive. He was a tournament tennis player in his younger years and…' Ann paused.

'And alcohol will only make things worse.' The priest completed the sentence for her. 'Can you get him to a doctor?'

'I got him to go to Hubert Bauer who gave him *Reserpine* for high blood pressure and put him on a diet. But I haven't seen much change… I think he's cheating on the diet.'

'How about a psychiatrist?'

Ann snorted. 'Not a chance!'

'I see.' Father Preston thought for a moment. 'We'll have to do something. Will you leave it with me for a while?'

'Yes, Father. You don't have any ideas right now?'

'I'm afraid not… but I'll be in touch with you.' He took her hand. 'Try not to worry.'

'I'll try,' she said, sadly. 'But I don't know how much more I can take.'

On the following Saturday, Ann was sitting on the front deck when she heard voices. Entering the living room she encountered George, Hubert and Walter coming in after their golf game.

'Come in… come in,' George shouted, 'this is the twentieth hole.'

Ann could tell that he had had several drinks at the nineteenth. 'Yes, do come in,' she added, 'I'll put on some coffee.' She went into the kitchen.

'Coffee, Bah!' George went to the bar. 'What'll you guys have?'

'Scotch on the rocks, please,' Walter replied. 'Excuse me…' he headed for the bathroom.

'I'll just have a ginger ale,' Hubert said, reprovingly. He was annoyed at George for ignoring advice on cutting down his drinking.

Walter returned and added up the score card. 'George—you owe everybody. Six dollars to me, three to Hubert and two to Jim.'

'I'm going to give up that damn game,' George said, irritated. 'A bunch of grown men chasing little balls…'

Ann returned. 'Where is Father Preston?'

'He'll be here in a minute,' Walter explained, 'he had to make a stop.' He picked up a photograph from the piano. 'Is this the new ·grandchild?'

'Yes,' Ann answered. 'The one you added to George's Will.'

Walter turned to George. 'How does it feel to be a grandfather?'

'I don't mind.' He smiled at Ann. 'It's being married to a grandmother that bothers me.'

'Oh, you…' she grimaced.

Walter picked up another photo. 'And this is Karen?'

'Yes,' Ann replied. 'She's a copywriter for an advertising agency in Toronto.'

Hubert said, 'I seem to recall that she had a husband—is she divorced now?'

'No,' Ann replied, sharply, 'her husband was killed in a car crash.'

'Oh, I'm sorry,' Hubert apologized. 'I just assumed… everybody is divorced these days…'

'Not everybody,' Ann remarked.

'Well, our divorce rate is forty percent,' Hubert said, pedantically. 'The younger generation have no morals. It doesn't matter if they are married or not; just hop into bed at the least excuse. Why, I never slept with my wife before we were married. Did you, George?'

'I don't know,' George took a large swallow. 'What was her maiden name?'

There were chuckles at this sally, but Hubert was not amused. 'Oh, you know what I mean.'

'Yes, I do,' George responded, 'and you're still back in the fifties. Times have changed and you haven't. Better or worse, we have to live in today's world so we might as well make the best of it.' He weaved to a chair and sat down; the others looked at him with narrowed eyes.

Ann interceded. 'I just wish it made the young people happier to live together before marriage. In theory, it should lead to fewer divorces but it doesn't seem to.'

'I agree,' Walter said. 'My three kids all played around before they got married, but at least they didn't have any kids. It's the kids that suffer when things break up.'

'Yes,' Hubert agreed. 'Birth control isn't as easy as most of them think.'

George put his feet on the coffee table. 'It gets easier as you get older. I'm like George Burns. When an interviewer asked him if he could remember the first time he had sex, Burns replied: 'The first time? I'm so old I can't even remember the last time!"

'George!' Ann reproved. 'Of course, older couples are breaking up, too… people who have been married for forty years.'

'The young people have it too soft today,' Hubert said. 'They want to start with everything that it took us years to acquire—cars, TV, cottages, vacations in Europe…'

'You mean,' George slurred, 'all the things we finally got when we were too old to enjoy them.'

'What was that?' Hubert cupped a hand to his ear.

George repeated himself but his words were now hard to distinguish. 'This work ethic handed to us by our parents is for the birds. We didn't have enough fun…' He lurched to his feet and headed for the bar. 'Who's for another?'

Everybody declined. 'Where the hell is Jim,' George demanded.

At that moment there was a knock on the door and Father Preston entered.

'Speak of the Devil!' George shouted.

'Consorting with the opposition, George?' the priest smiled.

'At my age,' George answered, 'one can't be too careful. Have a drink… the sun's behind the mountain.'

'Not right now. I've been running too hard today. I have…' Preston gasped for breath and took a small box of pills from his pocket. 'May I have a glass of water, Ann?'

'Of course.' She hurried to the bar. 'Here…'

He swallowed a pill and smiled wanly at the worried faces around him. 'It's not serious… just a heart that doesn't keep good time… I'll be all right now.' He sat down.

Walter said, 'George owes you two dollars from golf, Jim.'

'Put it in the collection plate tomorrow, George.' Preston paused. 'I will see you tomorrow? You haven't been all that regular at Mass or at the Sacrament of Reconciliation.'

'The *Who* of *What?*' George slurred.

'That's Confession, George,' Ann said.

'Good grief! I don't understand anything any more,' George said. 'Hey… speaking of Confession, here's a story for you. There was a middle-aged Italian fellow who was a roustabout, never had a steady job, lived by his wits. But he was a Catholic and went to Confession. The priest said: 'What sins have you committed since I saw you last?' 'Well, Father,' the guy said, 'I stole five chickens.' 'H…m…m…, stole five chickens, eh?' the priest mused. 'Yeah,' the guy said, 'but make the penance for ten and I'll get the other five on the way home."

The others laughed.

George finished his drink with a large swallow and lurched to his feet, swaying. Walter put out a hand to steady him.

'I say… steady on, old boy.' But before Walter could catch him, George fell onto the chesterfield and passed out.

'He's had far too much to drink,' Hubert said, severely.

'Obviously,' Walter commented, dryly.

'Let's get him to bed,' Father Preston said. The three men man-handled George to his bedroom where Ann took off his shoes, loos-ened his clothing and spread a blanket over him.

Back in the living room, Father Preston said to the others, 'Have a seat… we'd better discuss this situation…'

It was ten o'clock in the morning before George Dixon emerged from his bedroom, nursing a massive hangover. His head throbbed, his mouth felt like the bottom of a birdcage, and his stomach was in a state of total revolt. He was stunned to find his wife fastening the straps on the last of two suitcases, dressed for departure. 'Hi, I'm…' he started, 'what are you doing?'

'Closing a bag,' Ann replied, dryly.

'I can see that. You're going somewhere?'

'I'm going to Vancouver for a while.'

'To visit your sister?'

'Yes.'

'Is she in trouble?'

'Not that I know of.'

'Then why…?' George paused. It was hard to think with such a headache. 'How will you get there?'

'I've got a reservation on the noon flight.' She looked at George. 'I feel the need to get away for a while.'

'I apologize for last night,' George said, quickly. 'One over the nine… it won't happen again.'

'So you say. But it's more than that. You won't do anything about your health and go to…'

'Oh, I see,' he interrupted, 'the Kraut's been blabbing.'

'Don't call him that!' Ann said sharply. 'He's a good man who's only trying to help you. Why haven't you been to the hospital for your tests?'

'I hate the place.'

She shook her head. 'And you're completely ignoring Hubert's instructions about drinking.'

'He doesn't know everything,' George muttered.

'You're headed for destruction and you're too pig-headed to admit it!'

'That's your opinion. I think...'

A car horn sounded outside.

'There's my taxi.' Ann picked up her bags. 'Yes, George... do think... think long and hard!'

'When will you be back?'

'When I'm damn good and ready!' She stormed out of the house.

George watched her depart with a sinking feeling of dejection and slumped into a chair. What would he do now? Being Sunday, he knew that he should go to Mass, but he couldn't face it. He went back to bed.

By the following morning, George had recovered from his hangover and was wondering what to do with the long day that stretched ahead. He could practice some golf...

The door chimes rang. He answered to find Father Preston on the threshold with a large bag. 'Good morning, George,' the priest said, cheerfully.

Nonplussed, George could only manage a strangled, 'Hello, Jim.'

'I thought you wouldn't mind a house guest for a few days,' Preston said, 'while the rectory is being painted. Since Ann isn't here...'

'How did you know she was away?'

'Somebody talked to her at the airport.' Preston didn't have a very good answer to the question and hoped that God would forgive the white lie.

George seemed to accept it. 'Yes... well... okay... come in. You can have the guest room.'

Father Preston unpacked and settled in. George went to the course to practice, returning in the late afternoon.

'How was the golf?' the priest asked, as George came in.

'Not bad.'

'Did you pick up the groceries?'

'Damn! I forgot… I'll get them later.' George walked over to the bar.

'Did you have a drink at the club?' Preston asked, mildly.

'Just a beer.'

'Best to have just one now, then.' He paused. 'I think I'll cook a roast for dinner; that way we'll have some cold meat for lunches.'

'I didn't know you could cook.'

'Many hidden talents,' Preston smiled. 'Don't forget to take the garbage out.'

George stood to attention. 'Yes, Sir!'

In the evening, Walter Branscombe arrived with a bulging brief-case and said to George. 'Now, let's get down to business about my campaign to run for alderman.'

George was startled. 'I didn't promise…'

'It was implicit, old boy,' Walter interrupted, digging into the briefcase. 'Now, what do you think of this photograph?'

'Not much,' George replied. 'Get one taken that shows how you look now—not how you looked twenty years ago.'

'Good point.' Walter handed a brochure to George. 'And what about this?'

George read. 'There's too much about how good you are and not enough about what you are going to do for the people if you're elected.'

'Good! That's what I wanted to hear! You can do some research for me along those lines.' Walter paused. 'It might be better if I was a native—rather than coming here from Nova Scotia.'

'Oh, that doesn't matter,' George replied. 'Natives are harder to find in B.C. than Nazis were in Germany after the last war.'

'Right,' Walter said, moving to the table. 'Let's make a list of things that need to be done…'

George Dixon thought that his house was in a good state of repair but Father Preston seemed to find an endless number of things to be fixed. The men had their usual golf game on Wednesday. Walter and Hubert came over to make a bridge foursome on both Tuesday and Thursday evenings. Together with working on Walter's election campaign, time went quickly for George. But he missed Ann. On Friday afternoon, the priest was working on his sermon for Sunday when the phone rang. 'It's for you,' he called to George, who was idly looking at some music. Preston could not help but overhear the conversation when George picked up the telephone.

-'Hello,' George said.

-'Karen... how nice!'

-'No, no... we haven't split up or anything... she's just been spending a few days there.'

-'Soon, I hope.'

-'Father Jim is here while the rectory is being painted.'

-'How about you? Busy?'

-'You've been in Toronto for ten years! I can't believe it!'

-'Yes, Cabbagetown is a great ethnic village now. How are your TV commercials?'

-'No humour allowed, eh? Do you remember when we used to make up limericks on the spot, given a key word?'

-'You can?' George laughed. 'Okay... get ready. Shuswap.'

-'Too hard?' There was a long pause. 'Not bad... not bad. My turn? Okay. Sicamous? Good Grief! Wait a minute.'

-'All right. I've got it.'

'There was a young lady from Sicamous,
Whose reputation was totally infamous.
She had born with joy
Two girls and a boy
To fathers who were mostly anonymous.'

-'Thanks. I'd bow but I'm sitting down.'

-'Yes... I will.'

-'Thanks for the call. Bye.'

George said to Father Preston, as he hung up the receiver. 'That was Karen.'

'So I gathered. I heard your limerick. Did you just make that up?'

'Yes. When she first started to work at an agency in Winnipeg, we used to have contests on rhymes, jokes and one-liners. She said it kept her mind in high gear.'

'I guess she likes her job then?'

'She likes the pay... objects to the meetings, having to kow-tow to the sponsors and the fact that they won't let her use any humour.'

'Does she travel?' Preston asked.

'Not much in her job but she likes to. She says she is going to get a new boy friend and go to Mexico.'

'She's flexible.'

'Yeah,' George said. 'If you're young and open-minded—you're flexible. If you're old and open-minded, you're dithering and can't make a decision.'

'Yes,' Preston chuckled. 'Well... I'd better return to my sermon. Don't forget to take out the garbage.'

'Yes, Sir!' George saluted smartly.

Father Preston was not available for the Saturday golf game. Walter and Hubert returned home with George, after letting him have only one beer on the nineteenth hole. Entering the house, Walter said: 'How about I order up some pizza for dinner and then afterwards we'll have a game of bridge?'

'Sounds good,' George agreed.

'Yes,' Hubert added. 'Where was Jim today? When will he be here?'

'He had a funeral Mass,' George replied. 'He'll be along soon.'

Walter went to the phone. 'I'll order the pizza for an hour from now.' He saw George heading for the bar and shouted: 'Only soft drinks, George!'

'Oh, all right,' George grumbled.

'Hospital tests for you next week,' Hubert ordered. 'And don't forget...'

'Yeah,' George was resigned. 'You must have good rapport with the hospital. I suppose many of your patients are old like me?'

'Yes,' Hubert said.

'Just live on and on, eh?' George said. 'They came to B.C. to die and then forgot why they came.'

'Good doctoring,' Hubert said, smugly.

'Oh, balls!' George replied, sarcastically. 'You doctors have carefully built up this myth of infallibility but you're wrong as often as you are right.'

'Oh,' Hubert replied. 'I'd put our average at better than fifty percent.'

'You would, eh?' George asked. 'That's not what the pathologists say. But you've got one thing going for you—your failures can't complain, they are all six feet under.'

'Unfair!' Hubert protested. 'Unfair!'

'In fact,' George continued, 'all three of you have fireproof professions. You bury your mistakes, Walter gets his fee—win or lose, and Jim's failures just stop coming to church so he never sees them again.'

At this point, Father Preston entered, put down his briefcase and gave a large sigh.

'Tired?' asked George.

'A bit,' Preston admitted. He got a glass of water and took a pill. 'After the Mass, I got stuck for Confession.'

'Any good stories?' George asked.

'Now, George' the priest admonished. 'You know that Confession is confidential.'

'Oh, come on,' George exhorted. 'You can tell us—we won't blab.'

'Well...' Preston thought for a moment. 'This didn't happen to me and it's probably apocryphal but...' He collected his thoughts. 'It seems that a young priest in Quebec was hearing Confession for the first time. A lad came in and admitted to the usual minor sins of swearing, telling a lie and missing Mass, and ended up by saying that he 'Sang the Apple.' The priest didn't know what that meant but he was too shy to ask, so he just gave a mild punishment of five *Hail Marys*. Then two more young fellows came in, used the same expression and got the same mild rebukes. But when the fourth lad said it, the priest's curiosity was too great. 'What do you mean,' he asked, 'You Sang the Apple?' The lad replied, 'Oh, that's fornication, Father.' The priest's eyebrows shot up, he rushed to the door, threw it open and shouted: 'Let's have the boys' choir back in here!'

There was general laughter. 'I must tell that one to Ann,' George said.

'Have you heard from her?' Walter asked.

'No,' George replied.

'You'll be glad when she's back,' Walter added.

'Yes, I will,' George agreed. 'More and more, as the years go by, I don't like our being separated. Oh, Jim and I are coping all right but things just aren't the same.'

'She'll probably be home soon,' Walter said.

'If the airlines aren't on strike,' Hubert added, dolefully, 'or somebody doesn't put a bomb on her flight.'

'Hubert!' George exclaimed, 'are you ever a harbinger of gloom and doom!'

'That reminds me of a story,' Walter said. 'Did you chaps hear about the airline statistician who worked for I.C.A.O. in Montreal? He was concerned about flight safety. He calculated that the odds against there being a bomb on board an aircraft were very high, but the odds of there being two bombs on the same flight were astronomical. So he always carried one himself!'

As they laughed, George said: 'Hey! What is this? Two stories in a row! How about you, Hubert? It's your turn.'

'I don't know any stories,' Hubert said, ruefully.

'Well… think hard,' Walter said, 'maybe one will come to you.'

The door chimed to admit the pizza. Father Preston quickly set the table and made some coffee. Just as they started to eat, Hubert cried: 'I've got it!'

'Got what?' Walter asked.

'A story!' Hubert replied. 'Listen! A golfer on the P.G.A. tour was lining up a crucial putt when a bird walked across the green right in front of him. He aimed a kick at the bird and said, in a low voice, 'Fuck off!' But a little old lady standing at the edge of the green heard him. 'Now, young man,' she admonished, 'there's no need to talk to the birds like that. All you have to do is wave your arm and say, 'Shoo, Shoo'… they'll Fuck Off.''

George choked on a piece of pizza and the general hilarity continued throughout the meal.

Afterwards, while Walter went to the bathroom, George set up the bridge table. He and Father Preston were partners. To the priest, he said: 'It's about time we won. We owe them eight dollars, you know.'

'Yes, I know,' Preston said.

'Can't you call on a little divine intervention?' George asked.

'I'll try.' The priest made the sign of the cross as he sat down at the table.

With Father Preston staying in his house, George could hardly evade going to Mass on Sunday. Returning home first, he made a light lunch and set the table.

The priest was appreciative when he came in. 'Oh, that looks good! Thanks, George.'

'No trouble,' George said, as they sat down. 'There weren't a lot of people at Mass today,' he commented.

'No,' Preston replied, ruefully. 'Attendance is down these days. We haven't recovered yet from the violence of the sixties and seventies when the authority of all institutions was challenged, including the churches.'

'Well,' George responded, tartly, 'if the church would make some effort to satisfy its members...'

'Such as?'

'Oh, come on, Jim... don't be deliberately obtuse. There's a whole range of things people would like to see changed—married priests, women priests, abortion,—and the church won't budge.'

'But isn't that one of its strong points,' the priest argued. 'The next generation may not agree at all with the changes you're suggesting. The church can't change its policies every twenty years.'

'You changed the Mass to English.'

'Don't you like the change from Latin?'

'No, I don't. I used to be able to go to any country in the world and hear the same Mass. Not only that, they've killed the beautiful music—the *Gregorian Chant* and the *Palestrina*.'

'But the Mass is now much more understandable to the people.'

'Maybe they didn't want to completely understand it,' George continued, 'perhaps an element of mystery is important. Anyhow, there's no mystery when the priest wears a sports shirt and serves French bread.'

Preston was startled. 'Did that happen?'

'Yes... in California.'

'Oh, well... not here.'

'It's only a matter of time,' George said. 'The atmosphere is different now. These new priests with their bright new words that nobody understands—ecumenism, shared responsibility, liberalism. Half the time the Mass is led by a young fellow who makes up happy-time liturgies and wouldn't know a breviary if you put one in his hand.'

'Oh, that's a bit strong!' Preston protested.

'Is it? Shouting and swaying to a steel band isn't my idea of a Mass.'

'Well, that doesn't happen in my church,' the priest said firmly, 'and I want to see you there every Sunday.'

'Yes, Sir!'

'By the way,' Preston changed the subject. 'Something has come up that I need your help with.'

'Yeah?' George was wary.

'St. Paul's School has lost its Athletic Director; he took another job in Vancouver. For budget reasons, the principal has decided not to replace him right away. He's divided up the duties amongst the staff except for a coach for the boy's baseball team. How about you taking it on?'

'I don't know anything about baseball!' George said.

'You've seen it played and you've played many sports yourself... you won't have any trouble.'

'How old are these kids?'

'Thirteen and fourteen.'

'I don't know...' George demurred. 'What's involved?'

'They play a game or practice three days a week after school and sometimes there's a game on the week-end. You won't have to look after their equipment—there's a man to do that.'

'Well, I don't think...'

'George,' the priest interrupted, 'there are times when one's duty stands up and shouts at you. Here's a chance for you to help some young people. You have the time and the ability and there's a need. Now, how about it?'

'I don't even know the rules,' George lamented.

'I just happen to have a rule book handy.' Preston handed it over.

'Oh, all right.' George gave in.

'Good man!' Preston clapped him on the back. 'I know you'll enjoy the kids.'

'When do I start?'

'Tomorrow!' Preston said, cheerfully.

The next week sped by for George Dixon. In the few hours remaining to himself, he found himself back at the piano with new music spinning through his mind. Saturday arrived before he knew it and the golfers gathered as usual in his house.

Walter added up the score card. 'We all owe George, who had an 86 today.' He looked at George, 'Your game has returned.'

'About time,' George smiled.

'I can't owe much,' Father Preston said, 'I shot a 93 today.'

'Yes,' Hubert said, 'but you had a little help from above... I saw your ball bounce back on the fairway after hitting a tree.'

'To each his own,' the priest said, smugly.

'How's the coaching, George?' Hubert asked.

'It's hard work,' George replied, 'but they're a good bunch. One of them looked at my grey hair and asked if I knew Babe Ruth.'

'What did you say?'

'Said that I knew him well,' George laughed.

'You'd better be careful,' Preston admonished, 'remember what Karen said about kids believing everything they hear?'

'Yeah,' George agreed, 'I'll have to be careful with my jokes.'

As they continued to talk, Father Preston left the room. He returned a few minutes later with his suitcase.

George was surprised. 'Are you leaving?'

'Yes,' Preston answered. 'The painters are finished.'

'Well,' George said, 'thanks for everything.' He looked at his three friends. 'My life seems to have changed radically in the past two weeks. I think...'

At that point, the front door opened and Ann Dixon walked in. Her hair was nicely coiffed and she wore a new suit—blue with white trim. George thought that she looked lovely, although he could see that she was still moving stiffly with her arthritis. 'Ann!' he exclaimed, giving her a fierce hug. 'Am I ever glad to see you!'

'So am I,' Preston agreed.

'And me,' added Walter.

'Me, too,' said Hubert.

'How nice!' Ann exclaimed. 'George, you're looking very well.'

'I am!' George replied. 'Jim has been keeping house in your absence because the rectory was being painted. And I've taken on the job of coaching the boy's baseball team at St. Paul's. They're a great bunch of kids and we either play or practice three times a week. And Walter and I are working on his campaign for alderman. And my golf game has been improving and my hospital tests were negative and...'

Ann held up her hand. 'I know... I know.'

'You know?' George's eyebrows raised.

'Yes. Father Jim has been keeping me informed.'

'How did he...? Oh, I see!' George looked at his three friends, who were all smiling. 'It's been a conspiracy!'

'You might say that,' Ann agreed.

George looked at Father Preston. 'I suppose the rectory didn't really need painting?'

'Oh, but it did,' he demurred. 'It could have been put off for a bit but...'

'I hope the Athletic Director really quit,' George added, 'you didn't fire him, did you?'

'Oh, no,' the priest replied, quickly. 'He quit.'

George shook his head slowly. 'You've all done so much. I don't know...'

'Don't you feel much better?' Ann asked, 'being busy all the time and little drinking?'

'Yes, of course. I can see now...'

'And I hear that your music creativity has returned,' she continued.

'Yes, it has. I'm working on a song now that will probably be the closing one. The characters in the play have much the same disabilities as we all have. So I've used us as role models.' George went to the piano. 'Here's how it goes.'

Life Ain't Over Yet

For Jim:

My heart runs on with uncertain beat,
I'll soon be on my winding sheet.
Often I gasp, feeling ill
Grab a seat and take a pill,
BUT
Life ain't over yet!

For Walter:

Many times it's total panic
With matters agonizingly phallic.
I just know I can't carry on
While I run for the nearest John,
BUT
Life ain't over yet!

For Hubert:

My patients' words are seldom clear,
I have to cup my hand to ear.
Sounds recede, voices fade,
I must get a hearing aide.
BUT
Life ain't over yet!

For Ann:

I'll soon by *non compos mentis*
In torture from this arthritis.
Not mobile until noon,
I'll need a cane very soon.
BUT
Life ain't over yet!

For us all:

We've hair that's thin and mostly grey,
Teeth long feeble with root decay,

We can feel an extra chin,
It's so hard stayin' thin.
BUT
Life ain't over yet!

We will keep our sense of humour,
Tales of senility are just a rumour.
We have years left to live,
A richer world ours to give,
'CAUSE
LIFE AIN'T OVER YET!

Author's Note: This story started life as a stage play.

The Runaways

In the early days of the century Prince George had the reputation of a brawling, backwoods, lumber town. Its red light district flourished. In Albert Johnson's Northern Hotel men stood six feet deep in front of a bar 90 feet long. Bartenders worked twelve hours a shift and, although whiskey was only 25 cents a drink, liquor sales reached $7,000 a day.

Transportation was the sole privilege of the mighty Fraser River. Stern-wheelers braved the rapids at Cottonwood and Fort George Canyons. One such was the 'B.X.', one of the finest to sail inland waters. Her dining room could seat 50 and her state-rooms had steam heat, reading lights, wash stand, fan and were finished with red velvet carpeting and green curtains. Fully laden with passengers and 100 tons of freight she could work in waters shallow enough for a man to wade.

In 1914 the stern-wheelers faced extinction with the building of the Pacific Great Eastern railway to Vancouver, although service was so slow and erratic that the P.G.E. soon bore the sarcasm of 'Past God's Endurance'.

There was little government regulation and fortunes were there to be made by those with foresight, little conscience and some capital. One such entrepreneur was Henry Hanford who, with exorbitant profits from lumber and transportation, had an architect design a large mansion over-looking the Fraser River at the end of what is now Clapperton Street. Known as the Hanford House, it had some thirty rooms, ornate wood carving and a large balcony facing the river. It also had cramped and inadequate servant's quarters. In time, the Hanford family moved away and the mansion became a boarding house, fading into shabby gentility. As the city grew, the demand from boarders fell away and, in 1980, the house was converted into a Home for Senior Citizens. In 1999 it had twenty tenants and a staff of six, assisted by volunteers.

Most of the seniors had been in Hanford House for several years and regarded it fondly in spite of its numerous shortcomings. It had no elevator, many of the rooms were small, there was no air conditioning, the kitchen was hopeless, there was constant noise from the approaches to the new bridge for the Cariboo Highway and a sulphurous smell wafted from the pulp mill across the river. However, the staff were kind and caring and there was a family atmosphere in the place. It was home.

Great was the dismay of both tenants and staff on the morning of the 6th August, 1999, to find a new notice on the bulletin board in the downstairs hall. In bald terms it stated that Hanford House would be demolished in September and that the tenants would be re-located, if they wished, in the Excalibur Nursing Home.

Mr. Bloom, the manager, who had placed the notice, sat in his small, windowless office and awaited the expected onslaught. He was about 50 years of age, a little over-weight, bald and humourless but not without sympathy for his aged tenants who now faced a move that most of them would not want. 'The first person that I'll get,' he said to himself, 'will be Martin Falls… the frisky old goat.'

His predication being dead accurate, Bloom was not surprised when, in the late morning, the door opened without knocking and Falls burst in, shouting: 'What the hell is this, then? Tearing the place down! To build condos, I suppose?' His words tumbled out so fast that he was in danger of losing his dentures. Thin, scrawny, sparse grey hair—Falls looked like an angry rooster.

'Yes,' Bloom sighed, regarding Martin sadly. At least he had his dentures in; a week ago he had driven a volunteer to tears by accusing her of stealing them. 'I think they are going to build apartments on the site.'

'They can't do that!' Falls spat. 'It's my home. I've been here for five years. If you think I'm gonna move to that new Excalibur place you can…'

'Calm down, Martin… calm down,' Bloom held up his hand. 'You'll blow a gasket. What do you think I can do about it?'

'You can tell them to leave us alone!'

'You know that wouldn't do any good. I don't own the place. I'll probably be out of a job myself.'

'Well, I'm not moving and that's that!' Falls turned to leave. 'I'm going down to the Legion for a beer.'

Bloom shook his head in resignation. Eighty-eight years old and going to the Legion for a drink in the morning. 'Now, don't you get into trouble, Martin.'

'I don't have trouble… nobody messes with me,' Falls said, fiercely. 'I beat up my top Sergeant when I was in the Army and I can still do it!'

Bloom looked at Martin's hands, gnarled and scarred from years of work as a car mechanic and stiff with arthritis, and knew that it was all braggadocio. 'Yes, all right.'

'I'll be back for lunch and we'll see about this. Maybe I'll take up a petition.' Martin stormed out.

He hopped on a bus and got off at 5th Ave. Walking down one of the main streets he glared at a young woman in a skin-hugging mini-skirt and tight T-shirt; scowled at two drifters on a corner; looked sourly at the price of a haircut—$15; and frowned ill-temperedly at a dirty long-haired musician begging for money.

Marching into the Canadian Legion, he snarled at the bartender: 'A pint of Pale Ale and no conversation.'

The bartender obliged.

Bloom did not have a good day. Almost every tenant was upset at the news and didn't hesitate to let him know. Next to Martin Falls, the most irate was Elizabeth Trueman. Not surprising, Bloom thought, since she bitched about most things; it was she who kept sending her food back to the kitchen claiming that it wasn't cooked enough.

Martin Falls and Betty Trueman had adjoining rooms and were good friends. They secretly revelled in being known as the scourges of Hanford House, driving the staff to distraction at times. Instinctively they knew, without conscious thought, that it is the surly, irascible and paranoid that survive the rigors of old age; those who vent their frustrations on others rather than meekly submit to the many vacuous rules and regulations that could dominate their lives.

A few days later, Martin and Betty sat in his room drinking whiskey; he kept a bottle handy for 'medicinal purposes.'

'Do you know this Excalibur Home that they want to send us to?' she asked, sipping her weak drink. She was 86 years old, slim with abundant grey hair and had poor eyesight. Her regular features and peaches-and-cream complexion hinted at the girl who had been a vivacious cheer-leader in high school.

'Yeah,' he replied, 'it's a big, new place... about 350 seniors... big and impersonal.'

'But I expect it has more amenitites.'

'I suppose so.' Martin took a healthy swallow. 'But I ain't gonna live there.'

'But where will you go?'

'What?' he asked. He was hard of hearing but refused to wear a hearing aide.

Betty repeated the question.

'I think I'll go to Vancouver,' he answered, grandly. 'See the big city.'

'What? You wouldn't!'

'Sure I would. Wanna come with me?'

Betty floundered. 'Well... I don't want to move either... but... what would we do?'

'Find a place to live and live it up. Movies, pubs, Chinatown, Stanley Park for walks...'

'But what would our children say?'

'Well, we've only got one each. I've got Randy and you've got Dorothy. We couldn't tell them we're goin' 'cause they'd kibosh the idea. We could write to them after we got settled to say that we're okay.'

'Well... I suppose...'

Martin could see that she was intrigued by the idea of running away to Vancouver. 'Look... you think on it for a few days... I'll get a bus schedule and make some plans.'

'All right,' Betty nodded; a small smile played around the corners of her mouth.

Thus the plan to abscond was fomented.

Betty Trueman was attracted to the idea of an adventure, although she had some misgivings about travelling with Martin. After all, she had been born in England, her family emigrating to Canada when she was 14 years old. Her father had ranched in the Cariboo for several years but went broke in the depression and moved to Prince George where he managed the Credit Union. She had always wanted to travel but her husband, who had died in 1990, was not inclined to do so, preferring to stick close to his accountancy business. But Betty was worried about what her daughter, Dorothy, who lived in Prince George, would think, and do, if Betty ran off with Martin. Oddly, she was not worried about her health although her eyesight was poor and she had had a heart attack two years ago. Her instincts said: 'Go for it!'

A week later the couple met again in Martin's room. 'Well,' he began, 'there's a bus that leaves here at six o'clock in the evening that should be good.'

'When does it get to Vancouver?' Betty asked.

'At nine o'clock the next morning.'

'That long!?'

'Yep. Fifteen hours. But it's good timing. Nobody will miss us until sometime the next day. They'll soon find out where we went but by then we'll be lost in the city.' Martin's blue eyes sparkled. 'Are you with me?'

'Yes... I am.' Her voice trembled.

'Good! We'll go in a few days.'

'What about money?'

'The bus fare is $80.00—plus G.S.T.' Martin replied. 'We could each take a few hundred with us in cash. What bank do you use?'

'The Royal.'

'So do I. We can nip down there tomorrow. Do your pensions go straight to the bank?'

'Yes.'

'So do mine.'

'Except for O.A.P.,' Betty said, 'mine comes to Hanford House.'

'Yeah,' Martin mused, 'so does mine. We'll have to get them changed.'

'But,' Betty's brow furrowed, 'what will we do with all the things in our rooms—pictures, clothes, some furniture and all that? If the place is going to be torn down...'

'We'll just take what we need... say two suitcases each... and we'll leave a note for Bloom to get in touch with our kids to pick up the rest of the stuff.' Martin wondered what his son, Randolph, who also lived in Prince George, would think about that.

'I don't know…' Betty demurred, getting cold feet.

'Now,' Martin ordered, 'don't back down now… we'll have a ball in Vancouver.'

'How long will we stay?'

'Who knows… who knows,' he replied. 'As long as we want to.'

'I don't want to be away from my two grandsons for too long.'

'Don't worry,' he soothed, 'we'll have some fun and play it by ear.'

Since Hanford House had a rear door and a lane they had no trouble leaving unseen, Martin having arranged for a taxi to be waiting around the corner. They were silent on the ride to the bus depot, each immersed in their own thoughts. Betty was worried about her possessions, in spite of the note that she had left for Mr. Bloom and the thought of causing distress to her daughter. Martin was looking forward to the adventure. Both had butterflies in the stomachs.

The large seats in the Pacific Coast Lines bus were comfortable and they began to relax as the rolling Cariboo country unfolded alongside. Arriving at Williams Lake at dark, they waited in a coffee shop while the drivers changed. Through the night hours they slept; Betty fitfully as she nudged Martin when he began to snore.

In Hope they had breakfast and freshened up and from there into Vancouver their spirits rose as the city emerged into sky scrapers flanked by the coast mountains.

'Where shall we stay?' Betty fluffed her grey hair with her right hand. 'Do you know?'

'What's that?' Martin held his hand to his ear.

She repeated the question, wondering how often this was going to happen.

'Let's try to stay in the West end,' Martin consulted his accommodation guide. 'There's a couple of B & B places listed here that should be okay for a few days while we look around.' He paused. 'We could get a room with twin beds… I'm past this sex bit, are you?'

Betty blushed. 'Yes, I am.'

'Good... that's what we'll do.'

And that's what they did. Found a pleasant house on Bidwell Street, just a short walk from English Bay, which had a large room with twin beds and provided breakfast. After a rest in the afternoon, they strolled down Beach Drive to Stanley Park, both enchanted with the people, the scenery and, above all, their newly-found sense of freedom. Hand-in-hand they walked, commenting, gesturing, nodding in agreement, Betty even giggling while Martin played the dominant male.

In Prince George it did not take Mr. Bloom long to notify Dorothy Casson and Randolph Falls that their parents were missing and to have the police ascertain that the pair had taken the bus to Vancouver. But the trail ended there.

Dorothy and Randy met with Mr. Bloom in his office in Hanford House. 'Have you come to collect their belongings?' he asked.

'Yes,' Randy replied. 'I have a pick-up truck here.'

'Fancy them going off like that,' Dorothy sniffed, 'at their age.' She was a heavy-set woman, 49 years old, with a round face and her mother's fine complexion. 'They simply have no consideration for other people. I spend so much of my time looking after her and now she does this.'

Bloom didn't think much of this statement—he seldom saw her or her two sons around Hanford House. 'Well,' he remarked, drily, 'he can't hear but she can; she can't see but he can... so maybe they'll be all right.'

'They maybe all right for a while,' Randy agreed. His father had lived with him for several years before Randolph was divorced, lost his house, and Martin had to go into Hanford House, all the while complaining because his son had no children and hence Martin had no grandchildren. Now the garage business that Martin had built up over so many years, first in Vanderhoof and then in Prince George, would bear the Falls name no longer when Randolph, now age 54, retired. 'But at their age,' he continued, 'one of them will have health problems sooner or later—and probably sooner.'

'What can we do?' Dorothy asked.

'They said that they would write to us,' he replied, 'so let's wait a bit and see what happens.' He was a large, slow-moving man, not given to hasty decisions. 'I'll go to Vancouver if need be. Come on… I'll give you a hand with your mother's stuff. And don't worry.'

Betty and Martin were delighted with the many wonderful sights and scenes of Vancouver. They settled into a routine of spending an active day followed by a quiet one in Stanley Park where it seemed that it would take forever to explore the many trails, the zoo, the Aquarium with its underwater windows and killer whale shows and rides in a horse-drawn 'Tally-Ho' when they tired.

The city centre offered museums, art galleries, planetarium and observatory. Canada Place with its huge white sails and moored cruise ships and a ride in the glass elevator to the top of Harbour Centre. This particular day had been a 'Chinese Day'; lunch and a leisurely tour of the exotic shops on Pender Street followed by watching the Dragon Boat races on False Creek. Martin described the traditional costumes and colourful trimmings that Betty could not see too well. They returned home tired and happy.

Martin had negotiated a reasonable rate at their house and they had installed a small fridge and a microwave. The room was large and allowed for a sitting area at one end, two comfortable chairs and a TV set. They had both written to their children to assure them everything was all right but without revealing their address. While money was not a problem since they cashed cheques against their bank accounts in Prince George, they did want their Old Age Pensions. 'What should we do about them?' Betty asked.

Martin thought for a moment. 'Well, Bloom will have them for next week because they are addressed to Hanford House.'

'He'll give them to the kids.'

'Right. Here's what we'll do. There's a Postal Station on Davie Street. We'll get a Box there and the kids can send them to us, and other mail too, and that way we can communicate but they won't know exactly where we are. We can send a change of address for the O.A.P. cheques to go to them.'

'Oh, Martin,' she gushed, 'you're so clever.'

Actually, it wasn't all that clever a move. As soon as Randolph was informed of the Box number, he hired a private detective agency in Vancouver. They quickly found out the Postal Station, staked the place out and followed Martin home. Within a week, Randolph had the address on Bidwell Street.

On a Friday afternoon in late September, Betty and Martin were relaxing in their room after an idle day. He had his feet up, sipping a beer, reading the newspaper. Betty regarded him fondly; while he still got irritated at times, he had lost the crusty belligerence and surly aggravation that had been so characteristic a few weeks ago. Without acknowledging her scrutiny, he was aware of it. 'She's a good old stick,' he thought, 'who tries hard to please.'

'Know what I'd like to do?' she asked.

Martin lowered his paper. 'No… what?'

'Go down to Robson Street later on tonight and look at the action.'

'H…m…m…,' he mused. Action there might be plenty of on a week-end night. 'Why not?'

At eleven o'clock that evening they were seated at an outdoor cafe on Robson Street near Thurlow. Martin was drinking a beer while Betty had a glass of white wine. It was a warm evening but they both wore sweaters. There was plenty to watch.

Two girls paraded by—high heels, short shorts, halter tops, frizzled hair, too much make-up, roving eyes—their profession was obvious.

Young couples of both sexes, and with either, walked with arms around each other, pausing to kiss and fondle.

In plain view on a corner a swarthy, young man sold small plastic bags of some drug.

On another corner, a long-haired musician idly strummed a guitar; at his feet was an upturned cap for donations guarded by a small, scruffy black dog.

Betty was entranced, constantly urging Martin to: 'Look at this… look at that!' Even playing man-of-the-world, Martin was hard pushed to look blasé.

The climax came when a tall skin-head came by with a girl on his arm. He wore sandals, shorts, beads covered his chest. Earrings in his ears and his nose. Rings on all eight fingers. His head shone in the lights like a polished canon ball. His girl wore sandals, a mini-skirt and her hair was a flaming orange. Martin could not suppress a gasp.

The skin-head was at their table in an instant. 'Somethin' botherin' you, Grandad?' He rocked back and forth on heels and toes.

'What's it to you, punk?' Martin said, belligerently.

'We don't like bein' laughed at.' His eyes narrowed.

'Then don't dress like a couple of idiots,' Martin replied, not backing down an inch.

'Martin… I think we…' Betty started.

'Shut up, Granny,' the girl said, moving closer, threatening.

Martin knew trouble when he saw it. Without a wasted motion he threw his beer in the skin-head's face, pushed the table at the girl, grabbed Betty's arm and ran for the interior of the cafe, shouting for the proprietor and the police at the top of his voice. In the resulting confusion, the skin-head and his girl faded away. Martin ordered a taxi to take them home. Betty cuddled into her savior.

In Prince George, Dorothy and Randolph met about once a week to discuss their wayward parents. By October, she felt that something should be done to get them home before winter and before some disaster occurred. 'We know where they are now,' she said, 'and you said that you would go to Vancouver.'

'I know… I know,' he demurred. Randy meditated for a moment in his quiet fashion. 'I guess I could go down next week.'

'What will we do with them when they come home?' she asked. 'Neither of us has room to take them in.'

Randy gave her a side-ways glance. Dorothy and her husband had a large, four-bedroom house and could surely find a place for her mother if they tried. 'We'll have to find somewhere,' he sighed, 'if not that Excalibur place, then someplace else.' He knew that his father would object to whatever Randy found for him.

In mid-October Randolph flew to Vancouver, rented a car and drove to the Bidwell Street address, arriving in the late afternoon. The parents were not at home. He parked down the street where he found some shade and waited.

He reflected on how sterile his life had been—and still was! A loveless, broken marriage—no children—an acrimonious divorce—no meaningful relationship with anyone now—a drab apartment.

Then he saw Betty and Martin coming down the street. He slouched down in the seat so that he wouldn't be seen. They walked hand-in-hand, faces animated and happy, talking about the day spent riding the Grouse Mountain ski lift and swaying on the Lynn Canyon Suspension Bridge.

Randy's heart sank. Who was he to interrupt their idyll? What gave him the right to interfere with their brief times of pleasure? So it might end badly; probably would when one of them developed a health problem. So what? Let them have the few joyful moments left in their lives.

Randy started the car and drove back to the airport. He would return when he was needed.

The Little Girl Who Swore

The Comptons were an average, middle class Canadian family who lived in an average Canadian small city of half a million population. The father, Graham, age 41, was an insurance broker with an average income. The mother, Florence, age 38, worked at City Hall as a statistician; she averaged numbers.

Instead of 1.6 children the Comptons had only one—ten year old Alice. To offset this 0.6 deficiency they had Florence's widowed mother living with them—known simply as 'Gran'.

The Compton house was a split-level in a middle class neighborhood of paved driveways leading to a two-car garage which held two medium-priced cars. Front yards had lawns with two flower beds and one tree, Back yards held sand boxes, swings, a barbeque and occasionally a swimming pool.

Graham played golf to an average 18 handicap. Florence bowled with an average of 150. Gran knitted sweaters that were slightly below average—one sleeve usually an inch too long. Alice was pretty, precocious and a year ahead of her class; she was above average.

Thus the Compton's life style was placid and peaceful (as Canadian lives are wont to be) until the day they discovered that Alice had developed a decidedly un-average habit, in a rather alarming way.

One evening, towards the end of dinner, Graham aligned his knife and fork precisely in the centre of his plate (as all Canadians do) and adopted his parental role.

'Well, Alice,' he said, 'did you learn anything interesting in school today?'

'Nah!' Alice replied. 'Our science teacher was talking about shapes. Y'know, triangles and octagons and stuff, using wooden cut-outs. She couldn't even find the right one. She's hopeless! She couldn't find her ass with both hands and a flashlight.'

'Alice!' Gran usually made a point of not interfering in family matters but this was a bit much. 'You shouldn't use swear words.'

'What's wrong with 'Ass'?' Alice protested. 'I've heard you call some one a 'Silly Ass'.'

Gran was rather stumped for a reply. 'Well… it just isn't seemly for a young girl.'

'Seemly, hell!' Alice finished her dessert and stood up. 'I've got some damn home work to do.' She marched out of the room.

Gran looked at Florence. 'You really have to do something about that girl's language. Where does she get it from?'

'Has to be school,' Florence replied. 'She doesn't go anywhere else.'

'Maybe we should speak to her teacher,' Graham suggested.

'I don't think that would do much good,' Florence said, 'it's her peers that are using the bad language… not her teacher.'

'Still,' Graham followed up, 'if the teacher admonished her it might carry more weight than ourselves.'

'All right,' Florence gave in. 'I'll speak to her teacher.'

'Yes,' Gran added, 'and you must be very strict with her in the future.'

A few days later Alice came home from school to find her mother still at work and her Gran in the kitchen baking cookies. Alice grabbed a couple and said: 'I'm going over to Terri's.'

'That's fine, dear,' Gran said. 'What are you going to do there?'

'We're playing Monopoly. I'm way ahead. I've got her by the short hairs.'

Gran blanched. 'Alice… I wish you wouldn't use that expression.'

'Why not?'

'Well… where are your short hairs?'

Alice thought for a moment and then looked down at her groin. 'Oh, well,' she said, blithely, 'we've only got a few.'

Gran raised her eyes to heaven.

Both parents and Gran chastised Alice every time she swore but it had no effect. Florence spoke to her teacher but that had no results either.

One evening Florence raised the subject of dancing lessons. Alice was light on her feet and had a good sense of rhythm. But Alice said firmly: 'I'm not taking any friggin' ballet lessons!'

'Now, Alice!' Florence protested.

'What's wrong with friggin'? I didn't say the 'F' word, did I?'

'No,' her mother said, wearily, 'you didn't.'

Gran looked at Graham and raised her eyebrows. He got the message and took his errant daughter into another room for a talk. 'Now, Alice,… do all the kids in your school use bad language?'

'Most of them.'

'That doesn't mean that you should.'

'Maybe not.'

'You know, a wise man once said that people who use profanity are ill educated and do so because they don't know the proper English word to use.'

'Doubtful,' Alice retorted.

'Besides, don't you want to appear as a properly brought up young lady?'

'Who gives a shit,' Alice said, as she strode out.

Graham reported his lack of progress to Florence and Gran, saying: 'Maybe we should take her to a psychiatrist.'

'Oh, let's not go that far,' Florence protested.

'Maybe she'll outgrow it,' Gran said.

So, taking an average Canadian approach to a problem, they procrastinated.

Then, one day, Alice rushed into the house and shouted to her mother: 'I'm in love!'

'Alice,' Florence shook her head. 'Ten year old girls do not fall in love.'

'I did!'

'Who with?'

'I don't know his name yet. He just came to our class today. He's as beautiful as a Goddam movie star!'

'Now, Alice…'

'Well, he is.'

Two days later, Alice rushed in again and shouted: 'His name is Jason. We had a long talk and we're going for Cokes after school tomorrow. I've got him by the balls!'

Florence sighed in resignation.

Alice and Jason began to spend a lot of time together, meeting daily after school and doing their home work at Jason's house. It turned out that Jason's father was a new Minister to the community.

Alice stopped swearing.

'What happened?' her bemused Gran shook her grey head.

'I dunno,' her father replied. 'It's a miracle.'

'Love conquers all,' her mother said, thankfully.

Win a Million!

Acme Investments had its office on the second floor of an old, dilapidated building on East Pender Street in Vancouver, on the edge of Chinatown. There was no sign, either on the outside or in the hallways, to indicate their presence. The door to their office was always locked. The name 'Acme' did not appear in the telephone directory. The one telephone in the office was listed to N. Smith, connected to an answering machine, and never answered in person. Literature sent to prospective victims (and there were many) gave a P.O. Box number for replies—never an address.

It was therefore very difficult for disgruntled customers (and there were many) to get in touch with Acme Investments. It was the largest and most successful scam operation on the West Coast. Many of its targets were Senior Citizens. It was a 'Boiler Room'.

Behind the locked door a large floor area was divided into two distinct sections, although there was no physical separation between them. It was a dingy place. The bare wooden floor was scarred and rough. Three windows on the south side let in a meager light, through layers of grime and dirt. In the top corners of the large room were spider webs. The walls held a few old posters and a year-old calendar featuring a naked girl. There was no washroom.

In one area four young women worked at two six-foot trestle tables, sorting printed matter and stuffing envelopes for mailing. They were paid $20 an hour, always in cash and with no mention of any other benefits. A stamping machine was in constant use and staplers banged in discord. A copy machine whirred constantly. A coffee maker held an empty urn. There was little chatter as the women worked at their mundane and boring chores.

In the other area, six men worked at scruffed metal desks in front of computer terminals with various papers strewn around. Here there was some chatter, as ribald comments were tossed back and forth. Had there been signs on the desks, they might have read:

'Norm Smith—Manager'; 'Bob Driscoll—Lonely Hearts'; 'Vince Tosci—Home Employment'; 'Len Talbot—Charities'; 'Frank Clark—Lotteries'; 'Yves Pinard—Invoices'.

Norm Smith (a.k.a. Nathan Samuel, Nelson Saunders) was a large, beefy man some 45 years old with a red-veined face, heavy jowls, generous nose, balding pate and hard eyes. On this day he was engrossed in three tasks.

The first was planning for the Commonwealth Games to be held in Vancouver in 1994, one year from now. Advertisements had to be placed in Canadian Provinces and in the U.S.A. for : non-existent hotel accommodation—deposit required; phony Sky Train passes—only if paid for in advance; bogus tickets for popular events—large discount if ordered and paid for in advance. And so on.

The second was to look for new accommodation; Acme Investments never stayed longer than six months in any one location.

The third was to estimate the gross take of Acme for the year 1993. It came to $2.3 Million. His five men received a small percentage of the net but overhead was low. They would all be pleased—especially himself!

Smith glanced at his men to make sure that they were all busy. The ground rules were simple—bring in as much money as possible and do little, if nothing, in return.

Bob Driscoll (not his real name) was a thin fellow of 55 years who looked 65. His lined and weary face said that he had seen it all. He had recently spent four years in jail for conning Seniors and was now very cautious; any sign of trouble with Smith's operation and Driscoll would be gone. He operated the Acme Lonely Hearts Club. Invitations to join, fee $50, offered Personal Introductions to members of the opposite sex, computer selected. None were ever delivered—Acme simply pocketed the fee. Years ago, Driscoll had run a more sophisticated version of the scam that established correspondence between the customer and a make-believe 'partner' asking for money because he/she was ill and could not get to a bank.

Yves Pinard, a wiry, dark complexioned French Canadian of indeterminate age, was using a Business Directory. He was sending out invoices for material that had never been ordered or delivered.

Each invoice was tailored to a given Company, had a bogus G.S.T. number and looked very realistic. Many an accountant would simply pay the invoice without checking further. Once, in the U.S., Pinard had used this scam with the billing coming from the 'Mafia International Brotherhood'; twenty percent were paid out of sheer terror. But this would not work in Canada.

Len Talbot, a stolid, phlegmatic man, was writing charity solicitations. He was concentrating on up-scale neighborhoods in Victoria, knowing that one reporter was quite right in saying that: 'There is a lot of quiet money in Victoria.' His favorite name at the moment was 'United Appeal' because it sounded so much like 'United Way'. Naturally, a tax deduction receipt was promised. Naturally, none was ever sent.

Vince Tosci, a charismatic Italian with dark hair and black eyes, who did everything at top speed, was writing newspaper ads and direct mailings which stated that a person could earn up to $1,000 a week at home by processing mail. He, too, had spent a few years in jail for conning Seniors. Carefully groomed, smooth talking, confident, he posed as a police officer trying to catch a thief in the building. He would ask a Senior to check and make sure that all his/her money and valuables were intact. He then asked the Senior to go down stairs to view a person being held to see if he/she had seen him around the premises. While the Senior was doing this, Tosci lifted the money and valuables. But one day he ran into a retired RCMP fraud squad officer who nailed him on the spot.

Frank Clark (n.h.r.n.) was a round-faced chubby young man of 28 years whose rumpled clothes always looked as if he slept in them. He had a ribald sense of humour which kept the office laughing. He was working on a lottery that never paid any prizes. He called across to Len Talbot: 'Hey, Len... you got that updated print-out of Senior Citizens?'

'Yeah,' Talbot replied, 'I got it yesterday from Social Services.'

'Well, pass it over,' Clark laughed, 'they are all gonna win a million dollars.' That one of the names on the list was a Joseph Patchell meant nothing to Clark.

Joe and Agnes Patchell lived in a modest, two-bedroom, frame house in South Vancouver. The house badly needed painting and the garden was mostly weeds. Neither of them was inclined to do much work and money was scarce.

Joe, age 75, had grown up in the neighborhood. Never a scholar, he quit John Oliver High School in Grade Ten for a job in the lumber mill at the foot of Fraser Street. Agnes, his 'steady' in High School, promptly got pregnant and they were married in 1940; he was 22 years old and she was eighteen. The baby, a boy, was still-born and she could have no further children. During World War II, Joe served in Italy with the Canadian Army but did not advance above the rank of private. Agnes worked as a waitress.

After the war, Joe resumed his job in the lumber mill. He was a desultory worker, tending to drink a lot on the week-ends and be 'sick' on Mondays. He got fired. He then worked on a fishing boat but it was seasonal; he drew U.I.C. for the rest of the year while doing odd jobs. Agnes worked in a laundry and then as a ticket seller at the P.N.E. They managed to save enough money for the house down payment but it still had a mortgage. They both retired at age 65 when they could draw O.A.P.

Joe was convinced that the only way out of penury was to win on the B.C. Lottery. He spent $30.00 a week on tickets. Although he won only the occasional small prize, he was sure that it was only a matter of time until he hit the jackpot.

He was therefore delighted to receive in the mail a personalised letter which stated boldly on the front:

YOU—JOE PATCHELL!
YOU ARE THE ONE!
YOU HAVE WON A MILLION DOLLARS!

'Look at this!' Joe shouted, as he ran into the house, his pot belly bouncing up and down. 'I've won at last!'

'You have?' Agnes was not excited. 'What does it say?'

'Says that the computer has selected my name among the very few eligible to win a million dollars!'

'What do you have to do?' Agnes sat down heavily. She was some twenty pounds over-weight and wore a shapeless T-shirt and jeans. Her hair was grey but thick. There were few signs now of the pretty girl she had once been.

'Just a minute.' Joe reached for his glasses in order to read the fine print. 'My number is 76421. I have to fill in this slip with my number and return it to them—Acme Investments—in the envelope. And I have to send $7.95 for judging and handling.'

'H…m…m…,' she mused. 'Are you gonna do it?'

'Sure,' he replied, 'it's prob'ly better odds than the B.C. Lottery.'

A week later Joe got another personalized letter from Acme that stated boldly on the front:

GOOD NEWS—JOE PATCHELL!
WE HAVE EXPANDED THE LOTTERY
TO INCLUDE A NEW CHRYSLER, A TRIP
TO HAWAII AND A DIAMOND PENDANT

Reading further, Joe was informed that merely by sending another $19.95 his name would be entered for the additional prizes. He sent the money. He never heard from Acme Investments again.

A few days later Agnes asked, with sarcasm: 'Well, did you win a million dollars?'

'I haven't heard yet.'

'And prob'ly never will. You piss away all our money on lottery tickets and wild-assed schemes!'

'We'll win one day… then we'll be rich.'

'Oh, sure,' Agnes scoffed, 'just like that vending machine business that you put our money into.'

'That wasn't my fault,' Joe replied, hotly, 'how could I have known that my partner was a crook?'

'We never have any money,' Agnes was on a roll, 'if you ever had a decent job we would have some security for our old age.'

'I've worked hard all my life,' he defended.

'Yeah? At what? If you had any education…' It was a time-worn subject.

'Who are you to talk?' Joe shouted. 'You never finished high school either!'

'Because you got me pregnant!' Her face was red with fury. 'You big prick!'

'Too fuckin' bad,' he retorted. 'It wasn't all my fault, y'know.' He headed for the door. 'I'm goin' out for a beer.' The door slammed behind him.

Agnes sighed. He wouldn't be back for hours now and probably drunk as well. They hadn't made love in ages; his breath was so bad from his poor teeth that it put her off and he wouldn't have them out and get dentures like she had. She sighed again. What to do? She could watch TV or go to visit her sister who lived nearby. She chose the latter even though it meant changing her clothes.

At Acme Investments, Bob Clark saw the second cheque from Joe Patchell for $19.95 and placed a 'tick' beside the name. He was finished with Patchell. But others were not.

Vince Tosci had completed his write-ups for home employment. The newspaper ads were ready to be placed and the flyers and booklets had been received from the printers. One young woman, who worked exclusively for Tosci, had already mailed 1,000 flyers to a list that Tosci had obtained from a mole in the Vancouver Sun selecting names in the poorer areas of Vancouver.

Now, Tosci shouted at the office generally : 'Who's got the Senior Citizens print-out?'

'I have,' Clark responded.

'Well, pass it over… I'm ready to go with these work-at-home flyers.'

'What name are you using?' Smith asked, turning his hard eyes on Tosci.

'Shephard Corp., P.O. Box 639,' Tosci replied.

'Why don't you call it Shephard's Italians?' Clark shouted. 'Then your acronym could be 'SHIT'!'

Everyone laughed except for Smith, who was all business. 'You're not sending personalized letters, are you?' They were more expensive.

'No,' Tosci replied, 'they just go to the household. That way, anybody in the place might bite.'

'Good,' Smith nodded.

Since the work-at-home flyers were sent to the household, Agnes Patchell was the first to read it. It said that up to $1,000 a week could be earned by processing mail at home. Supplies were free. A stamped post card was attached for a reply.

When Joe arrived home from getting the car serviced, Agnes thrust the flyer at him. 'Have a look at this.'

'What is it?'

'A way to earn some money at home,' she replied. 'Even you might be able to do it.'

'Cut the sarcasm,' Joe growled. He read the flyer. 'Sounds okay... I'll send it in.'

A few days later a letter arrived from Shephard Corp. It extolled the money that could be earned at home by stuffing envelopes with advertising material. For a mere $29.95 they would send all the information to get started.

To forestall any further criticism from Agnes, Joe sent the money.

In response he got a booklet from Shephard Corp outlining the procedures for handling mail and how to operate a stamp machine. He was told that several companies in his area were looking for home workers. For a fee of only $99.95 Shephard Corp would send him a list of these companies and would also advise them that Joe Patchell was a steady and reliable worker who could be trusted to do a superior job. He would soon have as much business as he could handle.

Joe showed the letter to Agnes. 'What do you think about this?'

She read it over. 'I dunno. It's quite a bit of money. Do you think it is a fraud?'

'I don't think so,' he replied, 'they would have to get a permit from the Gov'mint to set themselves up in business.'

'Well...' Agnes was doubtful.

'I'll give it a try,' Joe said, firmly. 'We need the extra income.'

Vince Tosci noticed the second cheque from Joe Patchell and drew a line through the name. Tosci was finished. Patchell would never hear from Shephard Corp again.

Then Tosci thought for a moment. It seemed a shame to let such a fish off the hook. He walked over to Bob Driscoll whose lined and weary face suggested that he knew every scam ever invented.

'I've got a live one here, Bob,' Vince said. 'I know that you're working 'Lonely Hearts' right now but...'

'Well...,' Driscoll thought for a moment. 'I've still got all the stuff for Life Insurance for Seniors over the age of 70… no medical exam… no waiting… very reasonable fees.'

'Here's the guy's name and address,' Tosci handed over a piece of paper. 'If he lives for a while longer we'll get more out of him yet.'

Heartbreak

Margaret McLeod sat quietly beside her husband's bed in the Victoria Hospice while he died. His eyes were closed, his breathing shallow and raspy, his cheeks hollow and sunken because they had removed his dentures, deep lines on his forehead, his sparse grey hair uncombed. There was little left of the stalwart man that she had loved for so long. She wished that he would die but then immediately felt guilty as if she was thinking only about herself.

She took off her glasses, rubbed the bridge of her nose wearily, and shut her eyes. It seemed forever, these past few years of nursing Angus through his cancer. In the beginning it had been a routine operation for a cyst on the prostrate. Although it had been malignant, the doctors were confident that they had removed it all successfully. They hadn't. The cancer recurred and months of radiation and chemo-therapy hadn't resulted in a cure. Finally, in 1999, they said that it had spread to his liver, that there was nothing further that they could do, and that he had about a year to live. The year was about over and he had entered the Hospice four weeks ago.

Her reverie was broken by the arrival of her daughter, Jean, who slid into a nearby chair and whispered: 'How is he?'

'Nearing the end,' Margaret replied, twisting a rolled-up ball of cloth that had once been a handkerchief.

'What does the doctor say?'

'Tonight or tomorrow.'

'Oh, dear,' Jean lamented. 'How are you holding up, mother?'

'I'll be fine,' Margaret said, firmly. 'Did you bring Dawn with you?'

'Yes… she stayed in the car.'

'Twelve years old,' Margaret said, tartly, 'is old enough to face her grandfather's death.'

'You can't make them…' Jean's voice trailed off. Her pleasant, roundish face was normally blessed with a sweet smile and she looked younger than her 47 years. But now it was somber. 'Maybe tomorrow…'

'There may not be any tomorrow. Have you seen Robert?'

'I spoke to him on the phone,' Jean replied. Robert was her brother, older by four years. 'He'll be here as soon as school is out.'

Jean looked sadly at her father and sighed; he didn't look like her father any more. She glanced at her mother; grey hair, lines deeply etched in her face and thought, not for the first time, how strong she was for 83 years. Perhaps it was the Scottish genes; she had been born in Perth and had come to Canada many years ago.

While not dour, Margaret was certainly extremely practical and a perfectionist who had given her two children some hard times when they were younger. Now she sat stiffly upright on a hard-backed chair, showing little emotion, waiting for her partner of 61 years to pass away.

At five o'clock Robert arrived. He was a tall, well-built man with abundant dark hair now showing a few signs of grey. He was Vice-Principal of a High School in the Oak Bay district. 'Dad doesn't look good, does he? What does the doctor say?'

'Just a wee while now.' There was still a soft Scottish burr in Margaret's voice.

'It's sad,' Robert said, 'but I'm sure that he will be glad to be over the pain and to be in a better place.'

'Yes,' Jean agreed.

'And you, mother, will be glad when this ordeal is over.' Robert was seldom at a loss for words.

'Is Gerald here?' Margaret asked, abruptly.

'No,' Robert replied. 'He is at a critical time with his studies and can't get away.'

'Too bad,' Margaret said, drily. 'Neither of my grandchildren seem overly concerned with their grandfather's death.'

'That's not so,' Jean argued. 'I'm sure that they are thinking of him.' She paused. 'Were there any other visitors today?'

'No. I told them 'Family Only'.'

Jean nodded. 'This Hospice has been great, hasn't it?'

'Yes,' Margaret agreed. 'Everyone is kind and caring and they don't spout the meaningless platitudes that people usually say.'

'True,' Robert agreed. 'They have a wonderful attitude... calm, cheerful and amazingly straight forward about death and dying.'

'They just won an award of some kind,' Jean added, 'for best Hospice care.'

'They are giving me a room down the hall,' Margaret said, 'so that I can stay overnight.'

'They are thoughtful,' Jean said.

Jean left at six o'clock and Robert at seven. There was no change in Angus' condition when Margaret went to bed at eleven o'clock. Angus died in the small hours of the night when both body and soul are at their lowest. A nurse woke Margaret up without saying anything. Margaret knew. She sat by her husband's bed for a while, unable to stop the tears trickling down her cheeks. Yet she was glad that her, and his, ordeal was over.

The funeral was held a few days later and many of their friends attended, as did both grandchildren. There was no reception. Margaret said: 'The Irish have a drunken party when some one dies... we do not.'

For the first few days after the funeral Margaret was bemused and couldn't seem to settle down to anything. She hadn't really felt old until now. It was as if Angus' death had suddenly plummeted her into old age. Her arthritis was worse and when she got out of bed in the morning she moved stiffly. She seemed to lack judgement and have no ambition to get on with her life, although she knew that she must now plan for her future.

One of the nurses at the Hospice had told her not to think in terms of a loss but as an opportunity to travel, learn new languages, attend cultural events like plays and opera, and make new friends. The Hospice had even given her a booklet on the subject. But none of it felt real... maybe later... when she was better adjusted to the loss of Angus, for they had always done things together.

Jean and Robert had spent a few hours discussing their mother's future. They concluded that she should sell the family house and most of its possessions and move to a retirement home. Neither of them looked forward to trying to persuade her to do this. But they summoned their courage a week after the funeral and met at their mother's house in Esquimalt.

'Mother,' Robert opened, 'we have to think now of your future.'

'Yes, I know,' she agreed.

'Jean and I think that you should sell this place and move to a nice retirement home... there are many in the Victoria area.' He spoke quickly, as if trying to get it all out at once. 'And the sooner the better while your health is still good... many places won't take people if they are failing. Neither Jean nor I can really take you in...' His gaze shifted.

Margaret looked skeptically at her son. He had a large house in Oak Bay and Gerald was away at university in Vancouver. But his wife...

'We'll help all we can,' Jean said. 'I'll take some time off work.' She was a social worker for the Province.

'I think I'll go into Central Park Lodge,' Margaret said, casually, amused at the looks of relief on both of their faces. 'I was there a few weeks ago to visit a friend and it's a nice place.' She didn't mention that she had looked at several retirement homes and the one she liked best was the new Abbyfield Home which was a million-dollar mansion in Oak Bay. But it was very expensive and she was determined not to be a burden on her children.

Robert recovered first. 'I see that you have thought this all out.'

'Yes. I know that I can manage here for a while yet but soon I'll have to move so it might as well be now.'

'Quite so,' Jean said. Her house was not big enough to take her mother in. 'We'll have a huge garage sale and then get a dealer to take the large stuff...'

'One stipulation,' Margaret interrupted. 'This has been my home for forty years and I don't want strangers tramping through it. You can sell the place after I've moved.'

'All right,' Robert agreed. He was quiet-spoken but stubborn when his mind was made up. 'Do you want to keep the car?'

'No,' Margaret mused. 'I don't think so.'

'Okay,' he replied. 'I'll buy it from you and give it to Gerry.' He paused, his conscience troubling him. 'We don't have to rush into this, y'know.'

'Let's get started,' Margaret said, firmly.

'I'll pick you up tomorrow,' Jean said, 'and we'll have a look at

Central Park Lodge and see what they have to say. One thing we could do right now is to pack up Dad's clothes and stuff and I'll take them to Goodwill.' She looked at her brother: 'Can you find some boxes?'

'Sure,' Robert said.

On the following morning Margaret awoke full of resolve to get started on 'sorting things out'. Getting dressed, she opened the double louvred doors of the large clothes closet and reeled back in shock. It was half empty! But of course it was—hadn't she watched the children packing Angus' clothes and shoes last evening. She opened the drawers on his chest—all empty. In the bathroom, all of his shaving material, hair brushes and lotions were gone. She gave a little shiver—they could have left something—it was as if Angus had never existed.

After breakfast, she wandered around the house. Where to start? She looked at the pictures on the walls. My—there were a lot. She went from room to room—counting. Thirty-six. What to do with them all? The children would want some. She could probably take two or three with her but the decision would have to wait until she talked to the children. She looked at the two round-framed prints of Perth that had belonged to her grandmother, over 100 years old. She remembered packing them so carefully when she and Angus had come to Canada in 1938.

Although Angus had been a skilled millwright, the depression was severe in Scotland and he couldn't find a steady job. They de-cided to emigrate. Why to Canada? Well—several cousins and uncles had come years ago to work for the Hudson Bay Company and they said it was a good country. Why B.C.? Well—the weather was mild and not unlike Scotland. Why Victoria? Well—it was sup-posed to be an 'English' city.

Angus quickly found work in the Esquimalt Shipyard and in 1952 they had built this house on Beatty Street, just one block from the ocean. She would certainly take the two old pictures with her.

She looked at the TV and Stereo and wondered if either of them could be taken to her new place; she would have to ask about that. She looked at the 100 or so books that they had accumulated over the years. She would take a few of her favorites but she wasn't strong enough to lift and pack the remainder.

And there was so much furniture! She guessed that she would be able to take two or three small pieces. Like the Camel Saddle that Angus had used for a foot stool. She remembered when they had bought it—in Egypt. It was 1965 before they could afford a proper holiday. When Angus asked where she wanted to go, she replied: 'To Egypt... to see the pyramids!' It had been a wonderful holiday! She remembered how the people boarding the aircraft had joked with Angus about carrying the Camel Saddle aboard.

And perhaps she could take the antique wash-stand—it wasn't very large. When she had bought it, it had no water jug or bowl. She had instructed a local artisan as to colour and design and had them made. Angus thought the job a bit pricey! She would take it!

When she paused for lunch she found that she had not really done anything. Her intention had been to sort out things for the Garage Sale but there was no such pile. This was ridiculous! After lunch and a brief nap she would get at it!

Arising, she thought about her clothes—she had far too many— Goodwill could have some. She was again dismayed at the half-empty closet but resolutely got on with the job. She put some aside and then came to a tartan skirt—Stewart Tartan. She thought of the last trip that Angus had been able to take, three years ago, to Scotland. He had offered to buy her a skirt of the McLeod tartan but she had said, sharply: 'I'm not a McLeod... my family are Stewarts... I'll have their tartan.' She would keep the skirt even though it was a wee bit snug now.

Margaret went to the garage for a box in which to pack the clothes. She looked askance at the array of tools and garden implements— Robert would have to deal with them.

What else? She gazed at the several house plants, so carefully nourished. Perhaps Jean would take some. In the kitchen she thought of the many extra dishes that she had. Some could go but, again, Jean might want some. She put aside some of the older ones that nobody would want. Tucked away at the back of a shelf was a small, silver music box. She picked it up lovingly. It had once played a part of the Moonlight Sonata but its spring was broken and it would no longer wind. Years ago, Angus had found it in an antique store and given it to her for a birthday. She didn't know what to do with it.

At the end of the day Margaret looked with pity at the little pile of things that she had gathered for Goodwill and for the Garage Sale. She realised that she had to have help—she could not do it alone. Dejected, she sank into a chair.

She was tired but she hadn't really done much work today. All her life she had been able to cope with whatever fate had thrown at her. All her life she had been needed, first by the children and then by Angus. Now she was needed no longer. Was this how life would be now? Unable to do anything useful... empty... alone... un-wanted?

Time Zone

Francis Quarry chose to work at home that day. With his Personal Computer, LCD Monitor, PPF—560 Fax, Laser colour printer and cellular view phone it was not necessary to go into his office. As a Manager, he was one of the few people that had an actual office.

With the virtual office, clerical workers had to make a reservation for space; then they picked up a laptop and a phone from the receptionist and went to an assigned work area. These areas were laid out like living rooms with carpets, comfortable chairs and tables and the necessary jacks.

There were few distractions and by early afternoon Francis had done a day's work. He looked at his digital chronometer; he would have to leave soon. His mother was scheduled to die at 1600 hours and he wanted to be there beforehand.

At the Terminal Hospice, Jennifer Agnew was composed and resigned. She was 90 years old and very frail. Her affairs were in order; her will was made and aside from a few gifts to friends, all would go to Francis who was her only son. She had selected her time to die. Now, in 2065, the ridiculous ideas of keeping people alive on machines against their will, or keeping them so heavily sedated with morphine that they neither knew or cared about living, were long gone. People now made their own decision or, if incapable of doing so, had it made by their families. She would take her pill at 1600 hours; death would be quick and painless. Francis would be there; there would be no others since her husband was dead and her only grandchild, Aldo, away in the Mars Colony.

Francis Quarry's house in Mission was rather large for one person—plus his robot. He had had two female relationships over the years, with a son by the first, but he had no attachment right now. People rarely married these days. There was plenty of time for further affairs; he was only 52 years old and retirement was set at 85 years. His life expectancy was 110 years—unlike his mother who had been born in 1975 before tests at birth removed any genetic defects and ended disease.

It was time to leave for the Terminal Hospice which was in Vancouver. Francis reviewed his options. Since cars were not allowed in downtown Vancouver, it was not wise to drive. He could take his non-gravity skimmer but secure parking was a problem. Best to take the Sky Train which now ran to Hope; at 300 kms/hr it would take less than half an hour. He wore blue coveralls which denoted his rank and picked up a llama-wool sweater. The weather was always warm now because the solar discs directed sunlight where it was needed. Francis programmed his robot to complete the housework and to make dinner; the instructions could be changed at any time, no matter where he was, with his Spectrix Remote Control. He activated the Force Field around the house and departed for the Sky Train Depot, a short walk.

Francis sat stiffly upright in his padded, infinitely-adjustable Sky Train seat idly watching the Fraser Valley whisk below. His thoughts drifted. Often he went into a self-induced hypnotic trance when scenes from both past and future lives flashed into his mind. But this was not the time for that. He thought of his job as Assistant Manager of Robotics Inc., a firm that manufactured robots. He would have to chastise two of his men for improper work. Francis Quarry was a strict disciplinarian with little compassion and no sense of humour. He was in excellent physical condition with his H.E.M. (Home Exercise Machine) and his S.C.D. (State Controlled Diet), did not wear glasses and had no grey hair. He thought of the impending visit with his mother; he was fond of her although she had some old-fashioned ideas. He had never liked his given name of Rodney Agnew and changed it to Francis Quarry as soon as he graduated from Robotics Engineering School. He hoped that she would not be too sentimental.

Francis Quarry was startled at the change in his mother's appearance in the two weeks she had been in the Terminal Hospice. Earlier, he had wondered if she was ready to die. Now, there seemed no doubt. Her body had wasted away; face heavily lined and wrinkled; skin dry and transparent like parchment; brown eyes sunk deeply into ringed pits; hearing aids in both ears. She sat in a wheel-chair, an oxygen supply nearby, with her gnarled hands folded in her lap.

'Hello, Mother.' Francis looked around the room, noting two boxes placed neatly by the door. 'I see that you have everything in order.' He sat down in a chair.

'Yes,' Jennifer Agnew agreed. 'Most everything was taken care of before I came in here. One box is for Goodwill; the other is for you... some pictures and mementos.'

'All right.' Francis paused. 'Have they been good to you in here?'

'Oh, yes.' Her voice was barely above a whisper. 'They stay and talk.' She had been a nurse at one time and knew how brusque they could be.

'That's good.'

'And the Minister was in.'

'Did you know him?' Francis asked. 'You haven't been to church for years.'

'No... but he was kind and tender.' She looked at her son. 'You'll sprinkle my ashes in the sea, won't you?'

'Yes, I promise.'

'It's too bad we don't have cemeteries any more... I used to enjoy putting flowers on your father's grave and talking to him. He died in 2025, you know... you were only 12 years old.'

'Yes, I know.' Shortly after that the Council had decided to do away with cemeteries... land in Vancouver was too scarce and valuable.

Jennifer shifted in her wheel-chair. 'I guess it just added to the destruction of the family.'

'How do you mean?'

'Well...' she sighed. 'You changed your name... never married... only one child allowed now.' Her face saddened. 'Did you love Kala—Aldo's mother?'

'Well... I... Ah,' Francis was stuck for an answer; he had never really loved anyone. 'I certainly liked her a lot.'

'What about Inga? You lived with her for eight years after Kala.'

'Yes... I liked her a lot, too.'

'What happened to love?' Jennifer whispered.

'I... I...' Francis stuttered; he couldn't answer the question.

'I'll ask your father when I see him,' she added.

'Yes, do that.' Francis was relieved. He knew that souls met on another plane and were reincarnated. 'He'll be waiting for you.'

'It's all I have now,' Jennifer said, sadly. 'I think you should go now, Francis.'

'All right.' He stood up. He was relieved to see his mother so composed and serene. 'Goodbye, Mother,' he said, without emotion or any sign of grief.

'Goodbye, son,' Jennifer said, as he left the room.

Then she cried a little.

Break-Up

The Orchard sisters (not their married names) were quite close in spite of a ten-year age difference. They lived nearby in the Kerrisdale district of Vancouver and the two families visited regularly. They also had regular visits with their parents who lived in a condo near City Hall.

The younger sister, Barbara, was 30 years old and had two children, a girl age nine and a boy age eight. Barbara, who had married her childhood sweet heart—Peter Norton—had never wanted to be anything but a mother and a home maker. The children often came home from school to find the house smelling deliciously of baking and their mother, her round face flushed, singing in the kitchen. She always gave them a hug when they came home. They would tell her about their day in school and she would tell them a joke that she had heard on the radio, although she frequently forgot the punch line.

Carol, the older sister by ten years, also had two children—a boy fifteen and a girl thirteen. She regarded it as her duty to keep an eye on Barbara who, Carol thought, had probably been behind the door when the brains were handed out, although loving and generous.

Trained as a dental technician, Carol had the no-nonsense attitude typical of many nurses. She worked part-time and made sure that she and Barbara met once a week for lunch and had a family get-together with parents once a month. Her husband—Ed Jackson—was a realtor whose hours were flexible.

Although Carol exhibited a brisk, confident manner with no apparent worries, she was concerned that her two teenagers not fall prey to the many temptations in their world. She watched them carefully for any signs of drugs or alcohol.

Thus the Orchard sisters had reasonably serene lives in which 'Family' played an important part and this was impressed on their children. All was peaceful until the day that their mother invited them for lunch.

The Orchard parent's apartment on Broadway was undistinguished except that, being on the fourth floor and facing west, the view from the balcony encompassed downtown Vancouver, Stanley Park, the Lions Gate bridge and the mountains beyond. Although it was fall, the weather was warm and Muriel left one of the glass doors open as she prepared lunch for her daughters. 'Just a salad,' she mused, 'Barbara has to watch her weight.'

Muriel Orchard was a sprightly, vivacious woman—slim and attractive—who looked much younger than her 68 years. To her amusement, and Carol's chagrin, they were often mistaken for sisters instead of mother and daughter. Always neatly dressed, grey hair coiffed, Muriel still caused male heads to turn. She loved to dance and was a member of a square dance club although her husband, Len, refused to join her. One of the family stories, often re-told, concerned the time at a party when, in the early hours, the younger people were ready to call it a night, Muriel said: 'Well—let's dance!'

The daughters arrived together. After Muriel had been updated on the activities of her grandchildren and any other happenings, Carol asked: 'Where's Dad?'

'Up north with his gun,' Muriel replied, 'trying to kill some poor, defenceless animal.'

'Yuch!' Barbara wrinkled her snub nose.

'Yes,' her mother agreed. 'Let's eat… I've just made a salad.'

Conversation over lunch was steady and harmonious until Muriel dropped her bombshell. 'The reason I asked you both to lunch today,' she said casually, 'was to tell you that I'm divorcing your father.'

'You can't…' Carol blanched and choked on a piece of lettuce.

'OH, MO-THER!' Barbara wailed.

'But why?' Carol asked, when she had recovered.

'We've grown apart,' Muriel replied. 'We have nothing in common any more. Since he retired, three years ago, Len has done nothing but sit in front of the TV, watch sports and drink beer.'

Tears rolled down Barbara's round cheeks. 'But Mother… to get divorced… that's terrible.'

'Pull yourself together, Babs,' Muriel ordered. 'What's so terrible about getting divorced? People do it all the time.'

'Not at your age,' Carol remarked drily.

'What's age got to do with it?' Muriel asked.

'It's... it's... obscene, that's what it is.' Barbara mopped up her tears.

'Don't be absurd,' Muriel said sternly. 'Your father and I never do anything together any more. I like the theatre, arts and dancing—he doesn't like any of those. All he wants to do is to get drunk with his old cronies from the Hudson Bay where he worked all his life and,' she added, snidely, 'rose to the exalted position of Assistant Manager of the Hardware Department. All he ever wanted to do was to get his pay on Friday and wait to win the Lottery. Mistakes inertia for stability.'

'Does Dad know about this?' Barbara asked.

'No,' Muriel answered. 'I'll tell him when he gets back.'

'What will you do?' asked the ever-practical Carol. 'Will you move out?'

'Yes,' Muriel said. 'I may move in with Victor Muracci.'

'WHO IS VICTOR MURACCI?!' Barbara was in danger of coming apart.

'A man I met square dancing.' Muriel fluffed her hair with her right hand. 'I may be in love with him.'

Carol gave a long sigh. 'What does he do for a living?'

'He's a contractor,' Muriel replied. 'He has a large condo in one of those new buildings in the West End.'

'How old is he?' Carol added.

'Forty-five.' Muriel's blue eyes sparkled as she watched the consternation on both faces.

'FORTY-FIVE!' Barbara cried. 'Why can't you pick someone your own age?'

'Because men my age are stale and weary,' Muriel replied, 'and they aren't any fun.'

'And fun is what you want from life?' Carol asked, sternly.

'Why not?' Muriel looked at her eldest daughter. 'Why shouldn't I have some fun in the time I've got left?'

Carol had no answer to the question; yet she was greatly disturbed. 'You are breaking up the family and you are the one who always told us how important the family is. What will we tell our children?'

'Tell them the truth,' Muriel answered. 'They will still have grandparents... I'm not dying... although Len and I may have to visit at different times.'

'But what will people say?' Barbara said, sadly.

'Who the hell cares?' Muriel replied, blithely.

In the Norton household, Barbara held the family together at the dinner table and broke the news, trying to keep from crying.

Her husband, Peter, threw his hands up in the air and said: 'Incredible!'

'Wow!' exclaimed Grant, age eight, 'now she'll be able to join the 'Swinging Grannies'.'

'That's 'Raging Grannies', stupid,' corrected Susan, from the superior wisdom of her nine years.

'Whatever,' Grant said, blithely.

'I'll still love them,' Susan said, 'even if they split up.' She paused. 'But it won't be the same, ever again.' She leant against her mother.

Barbara's tears started. 'How could she do this to us?'

'Now, Babs,' Peter mollified, 'it isn't the end of the world.'

'Will Granny get married again?' Grant asked.

'She might,' Barbara dried her eyes.

'If she does, we'll have two Grand-Dads,' said Grant. Then, ever practical, added: 'We'll get more presents at Xmas.'

'Oh, Grant!' Barbara mumbled. She pulled herself together. 'We'll just have to ride out the storm and ignore what people say.'

But Barbara felt betrayed. It was as if her mother had deliberately set out to destroy the Orchard family and negate all the years of building the solid foundations nurtured by traditions. Her actions were foolhardy, reckless and could only lead to more trouble in the future for everyone.

Barbara dried her tears and squared her shoulders. She would be stalwart and brave through this crisis and would protect her family—fiercely.

In the Jackson household, Carol also broke the news over dinner. Her husband, Edward, although normally quite voluble, raised his eyebrows and said nothing.

'Will Gran get married again?' asked Ellen, age thirteen.

'Perhaps,' Carol replied.

'But we'll still be able to see them,' asked Andrew, age fifteen, 'won't we?'

'Of course,' Carol answered, 'but maybe not at the same time.'

'Will Grandpa be very sad?' Ellen asked.

'I guess so,' Carol sighed. 'He doesn't know anything about it yet... he'll still up north, hunting.'

'Wait until I tell the kids at school!' Andrew exulted. 'Wow! A Granny her age getting divorced!'

'Andy!' his sister chastised. 'You don't have to broadcast it to the whole world.'

'I'll just tell my close friends.'

'Oh, you...' Ellen snarled.

Carol caught her husband's eye and shook her head sadly. She realised that her mother had her own life to live and should not be expected to base her decisions on her family reactions. But, like Barbara, Carol felt betrayed. It was as if, with utter abandon, Muriel had torn apart the larger family and left Carol with the shards.

Muriel Orchard moved in with Victor Muracci and filed for divorce. At last reports, she's having a ball!

Clayoquot Sound

On the west coast of Vancouver Island the towns of Tofino and Ucluelet, eight kilometres apart, are separated by the dense forest of Pacific Rim Park and the majestic, sandy sweep of Long Beach where the huge waves crash along the shore after their endless journey across the Pacific Ocean.

Teaming with wild life both on and off shore, backed by virgin stands of red cedar and hemlock, the area is a natural playground which attracts thousands of tourists a year to its beauty although the NDP Government denied the area to poor people by charging admission.

South of Tofino is a place that the locals call the 'Black Hole'. The mountain-side beyond was clear cut in the mid-1980s and then burned to allow for natural regeneration. But no regeneration has taken place; the shattering eyesore is still littered with charred stumps and debris—a mute testimony to incredibly poor logging practice.

> *It is here, by the scarred roadside, that the protesters have made their camp, determined that the rape of the mountain behind them shall not be repeated at Clayoquot Sound; determined that the dense, lush woods of red cedar, balsam, spruce and hemlock shall remain a home to the wide variety of exotic plants and animals that it now nurtures.*
>
> *A few tents are in place for those staying overnight. Cooking fires prepare meals from locally donated food. There are no tables. Just a few folding chairs. Protest signs are scattered about. Most of the protestors are from B.C. but there are several who, just a few days ago, had been at an Indian blockade in Ontario; nobody seems to know who had paid their way to come to this remote spot in B.C.*

It is a cool, drizzly day and the demonstrators, mostly young, are wearing a variety of sweaters and jackets. Their mood is somber. Some are already awaiting trial. Some will not risk being arrested but will just help out in a minor role. They are preparing for the blockade tomorrow morning at the bridge spanning the Kennedy River over which the logging trucks must pass to get to Clayoquot Sound. Among the protesters is David White, 72 years old and in poor health.

After the war, during which he served in the Navy in the Pacific but saw little real action, David White used his serviceman's credits to attend Teachers College in Nanaimo where he had been born and raised. An idealist and a nature lover, his passions were molding the minds of youngsters and hiking the trails around Long Beach— years before it had been proclaimed a Provincial Park. On one of his hikes he met a dark-haired, friendly young lady who shared his love of the wilderness. Her name was Pat Smith and she lived in Port Alberni. To woo her, David moved to a school there. They were married in 1951 and their only child, Thomas, was born in 1953. Similar interests in reading, music and the outdoors made for a happy marriage which continued until her death in 1987 of a heart attack; the same year that David retired from teaching.

When his mother died, Tom White added a wing on to his house in Alberni for David to live in. His pension was not large and after a mild heart attack in 1988 he grew frail and was susceptible to colds and flu. The wing had a sitting room, bedroom, bath and a small kitchenette with a microwave. David usually ate supper with the family, but the meals were often not harmonious because there was little in common between father and son.

From an early age, Tom's only interest seemed to be in cars. By age 16 he had stripped and rebuilt his own jalopy and started drag racing around the island. Finishing High School, with no interest in further education, he started work in a garage and continued drag racing. Finally, in 1982, seeing no other future for his son, David financed Tom to buy a car and truck used-parts concern. By

1993 it was a steady business with four employees and an inventory of $250,000. Married to a childhood sweetheart, Catherine Roberts, they now had two sons: Mark, age six and Orval age five.

David was preoccupied with the demonstrations at Clayoquot Sound and supported them fully. But Tom's business depended on the logging industry, truck parts being his largest source of income. David would remark 'I see they arrested 19 people yesterday,' and the battle would be joined.

'Stupid bastards!' Tom raged. He was a large, bluff man with big hands and a generous paunch from drinking beer. 'They come from the cities and Back East and try to tell us what to do with our forests.'

'It's their country, too,' David said, mildly.

'They don't live around here. They get paid by Sierra and Greenpeace; when they finish, they'll go back home and get ready to protest somewhere else.'

'Not all of them,' David argued. 'Many are local people who are concerned about the environment.'

'They don't give a shit about our jobs,' Tom replied, taking a swig of beer, 'nor about our wives and kids.'

'Right,' Catherine, who always supported her husband, agreed. At age 38 she was a bit over-weight and saved from being pretty by a receding chin and a large nose. 'What would happen to us—and your grandchildren—if Tom's business goes bust?'

'Yeah... and I can't do nothing about it,' Tom added.

David winced at his son's grammar but made no reply.

Tom turned to his sons. 'If you kids are finished your dinner, go and watch TV.' Mark and Orval, uninterested in the grown-up argument, scampered away. 'But,' Tom continued, 'they bring in Robert Kennedy and call us the 'Brazil of the North.' What the hell does a rich guy like him know about working six days a week for a living like I do?' He took another swig of beer. 'Besides, there's lots of forest left around B.C.... just drive around the Province... nothin' but fuckin' trees.'

'Not rain forest,' David argued. 'And surely you don't agree with clear cutting?'

'No... but the gov'ment will make Mac-Blo change their ways, use helicopters to get the logs out and not drag them over the ground.'

'I wonder,' David said, 'now that Premier Harcourt has bought $50 Million of Mac-Blo shares, making the N.D.P. the largest shareholder.' He paused. 'I haven't seen any helicopters around, have you?'

'No,' Tom admitted, 'but there will be... the Clayoquot Indians will see to that.' He took a swallow of beer and chortled: 'Harcourt sure pulled the rug out from under your protesters by doing a deal with the Indians!'

'It won't stop the protesters,' David said, firmly, 'and I'm going to be one of them.'

'What!?' Catherine exclaimed.

'Go ahead.' Tom's brow lowered. 'Get yourself roughed up and put in jail... see what good it'll do.'

It is 5:30 A.M. and, while the sky is brightening a little, no sun yet penetrates the fog and drizzle over Clayoquot. The cold dampness seeps into the bones of some 50 demonstrators at the bridge over the Kennedy River. Some are huddled around a meager fire which gives little warmth. Most are young but there are a few oldsters like David White. Their sweaters and jackets are not warm enough for the piercing damp cold and they shiver.

They form a circle around Deborah Zerman, a 23-year old sociology student from U.B.C. who is the blockade coordinator. In a clear voice, she explains what will happen.

'We will form up in front of the bridge with our signs. An official from Mac-Blo will read the court injunction. Not too much noise or disrespect, please, because the courts will be tougher. Stay in place until the R.C.M.P. arrive. Those of you willing to be arrested,' she paused and looked at the older people, 'join arms, go limp and make the police drag you away.'

David White is among those willing to be arrested.

At 6:00 A.M. the first logging truck slowly approaches the bridge. The court injunction is read. None of the protesters move and some of the younger ones begin to chant, sing and wave their signs.

Then the process-server intones: '... and you people should be off the road before the truck stops.'

Nobody moves. David White links his arm firmly with the young man next to him; they smile nervously at each other.

Two R.C.M.P. vans roll up and twelve officers begin to disperse the crowd, explaining that they are breaking the law. Two of them manhandle David White and carry him away, one of them remarking: 'Come along, Grandad… off to jail.'

After ten protesters have been arrested, the daily ritual is over, bringing the total to date to 180. By 6:30 A.M. the logging vehicles, including an explosives truck and six huge rigs, rumble across the bridge and into the fog.

The R.C.M.P. vans carry those arrested to the jail in Alberni.

The District Court judge in Port Alberni, Mr. Webster, was in a brisk, no-nonsense mood and started court promptly at 9:00 A.M. He had 32 protesters to sentence and he was determined to get them all away today. They had all pleaded 'Not Guilty' to violating an injunction but obviously they were all guilty. They ranged in age from 20 to 76 years; half were male and half female; most were in good health but some were not.

Webster listened to each story and handed out sentences accordingly; none were harsh. He felt sorry for David White, who had a bad cough and looked very frail. Jail would not be suitable so the judge offered 21 days at home on an Electronic Monitoring System. David accepted. He would rest, he thought, and work on his book about early days in Port Alberni that he had started some time ago.

But the EMS turned out to be far from satisfactory. His anklet transmitted to a black box attached to the telephone which in turn relayed a signal to the Suretrac computer. But the range of the anklet was limited and there was no phone in his suite. This meant that he had to spend most of his time in his son's part of the house. He could arrange to go out for a doctor's appointment and the like but, aside from that, was expected to be within range of the phone at all times; a Suretrac car with monitoring equipment was apt to drive by at any time to check on him. None of the family liked the arrangement.

On a typical morning Tom would go to work early; Mark, in Grade one, would be off to school; Catherine would do house work and Orval would play around. David moved a desk close to the phone and either wrote letters or worked on his book. In the afternoon, Orval went to kindergarten and Catherine either went shopping or to the hospital where she worked as a volunteer. David was left alone.

He looked around the living room with sadness and resignation. There was not a book in sight—only a few magazines. There was no stereo or hi-fi—no source of music. No painting graced the walls, just a few mediocre prints and a stylized drawing of a racing car.

He knew that the monster 27-inch TV would be turned on as soon as Catherine came home and remain on until they went to bed. How could they live without any intellectual stimulation? How could Tom, raised in an atmosphere of erudition, with books and music everywhere, now completely disregard these finer things of life? David doubted that Tom even had a library card and his grammar was terrible. Also, he had no love of nature and in spite of living in an ecological paradise, paid no attention to it. Bowling on Thursday night and drinking beer with his cronies seemed to be the height of his aspirations. David wondered where he had failed.

Would his grandchildren grow up in an intellectual wilderness? Now that they were starting to read, he bought them picture books and would continue with boy's stories and deeper reading as they grew older. But would they read if they never saw their parents reading? All he could do was try.

By the end of David's 21-day sentence, nerves in the White household were frayed. Tom said: 'Well—you get your anklet off tomorrow. Is that gonna be the end of this nonsense?'

'What nonsense?' David asked, knowing full well what his son meant.

'You know what I mean,' Tom retorted. 'You can't go hanging around in the cold and damp, you've been sick ever since. And what good did it do?'

'It had some effect. Over 300 people have now been arrested and the courts are jammed. Just the other day Harcourt announced a further reduction in the logging of the rain forest south of Ucluelet. So it's worthwhile.'

'You may think so,' Tom said, darkly, 'but my business is falling off.'

'You're still making money, aren't you?'

'Just barely.'

'What will happen in the future?' Catherine asked. 'Will things get better or worse?'

'I don't know,' David admitted.

'Are you gonna keep up with your fuckin' protests?' Tom asked, harshly.

'I don't know that, either.' David replied.

His dilemma was unspoken. He didn't like living with his son and daughter-in-law because they had so little in common with him. Yet they had been very kind to build a suite for him to live in. His pension was small and if he moved he would only be able to afford very poor accommodation. And he would lose any chance to influence the upbringing of his grandchildren.

The only decision that David White came to was to have a phone installed in his suite in case he had to go on the EMS again.

Penny

She was just an ordinary dog. She was two years old and her name was Penny. Her luxurious black coat, silky ears and gold stockings suggested that her mother had been a Gordon Setter. But legs a bit too short, body a bit too stocky and curved tail a bit too long, hinted that her father might have been a travelling salesman. Her large eyes were a deep brown and very intelligent; her vocabulary excellent. She was a good watch dog and barked when anyone approached the house although she had a disconcerting tendency to roll over on her back for a tummy-scratch after a kind word or two. She was a 'one-person' dog and, even in a prone position, thumped her tail when her owner approached. Her owner was an elderly man named Charles Edmunds.

Charles Edmunds was 74 years old and not in the best of health. He had lived in Penticton all his life. When World War II broke out in 1939, he had just finished high school. He immediately joined the Army and was in the first division to be sent to England. After D-Day, he saw action with an Artillery Regiment and rose to the rank of Sergeant. Returning home in 1945, he was at a loss as to what to do. No scholar, he rejected the idea of university. After a variety of jobs in the lumber industry, he was hired to work in a hardware store in Penticton. The job suited him. He was a steady and diligent worker, neither ambitious nor competitive, friendly and helpful to his customers. There he stayed until he retired at age 65 in 1985.

Mutual attraction to one of his pretty customers—Sarah Garrett—led to their marriage in 1950. Although they never had children, it was a good union and they both had many relatives in the area. Charles was badly shaken when Sarah died of cancer in 1993. He still lived in the house on Dynes Ave. that they had bought in 1970. It was a modest, two-bedroom, wooden-frame bungalow just a block from Riverside Park on Okanagan Lake. Charles had paid $48,000 for the property; his last tax assessment evaluated the house at $50,000 and the lot at $150,000. But he was not inclined to move.

In 1990 a stroke had partially paralysed him down the left side of the body. With limited use of his left arm, he could no longer drive a car. However, his legs were all right and he could walk a fair distance, if slowly. He was thin, wiry, with sparse white hair and a face quilted with wrinkles and pain lines. One of the few pleasures in his lonely life was walks along the shore of Okanagan Lake.

Charles had day care help twice a week. A few months after Sarah's death, the day care helper—a friendly young woman—suggested that he get a dog to keep him company. Charles had thought about this a few times but taken no action. Now he watched the daily paper until he saw an advertisement by a couple who were moving to a condo where pets were not allowed and would give their dog to a good home. Thus he acquired Penny.

Penny quickly changed Charles' life. She inspected the large, fenced yard with approval, spraying a little scent here and there to define her property. In the house, she explored all the rooms and, after a few days, decided that her sleeping mat should be placed at the foot of his bed. Her food and water were established in the kitchen near the stove. In the living room her toy box gradually accumulated such things as a ball, clothes, sticks, a plastic bottle and a rubber duck. Her teddy bear became a constant companion and, as she had a 'Soft Mouth', did not get torn.

Since Penny was a young and vigorous dog, two walks a day became the norm along the lake shore. Charles also usually took her with him when ever he had chores to do in town. On the rare occasion that he left her alone in the house, he was always saddened by the sorrowful look in her brown eyes but delighted at the ecstatic welcome on his return when she danced about and wriggled her entire body with pleasure. Penny was always groomed to perfection and her lustrous black coat often evoked comments on their daily walks. She was always at his side; if Charles moved into the den to watch TV Penny came along, always willing to have her ears scratched or her back stroked and trying to wash his face with her large, wet tongue. They became inseparable friends.

Then came the day when Penny went missing. On the few times that Charles didn't take the dog with him, he usually left her in the house. However, this day was sunny and warm and, since he wouldn't be away long, he left her in the yard. When he returned home the dog was gone, a loose board in the fence showing where she had escaped.

For the remained of that day, Charles searched the neighborhood and the lake shore, asking people if they had seen Penny, becoming increasingly worried as there was no sign of his pet. By night-fall he was exhausted, pain intensifying in his side, discouraged and tormented.

Penny had two tags on her collar. One was her licence; the other was a vet's tag with his name and phone number showing the date of the dog's last vaccination. Charles phoned the Dog Pound and the Vet to inform them that Penny was missing. He then placed advertisements in the newspapers in Penticton, Kelowna and Oliver. He continued his search on foot but to no avail.

Days passed. Charles grew more despondent as there were no results from any of his efforts. His house seemed like some strange, alien place devoid of life. He threw away her dog food that had spoiled, remembering how she looked quizzically at the cupboard when she was hungry and how she brought him a shoe when it was past time for a walk. Where was she? Was she hurt? Had she been dog-napped? Would she ever return?

On the fifth day of Penny's disappearance, at eleven o'clock in the morning, the telephone rang. Charles snatched up the receiver. 'Yes?'

'Is that Mr. Edmunds?' The voice was that of a young man—rather rough and uncultured.

'Yes, it is.'

'I think I got your dog.'

'You have!?' Charles' heart leaped.

'Yeah. My name is Ben Volker and I live in Oroville in Washington. The dog was wandering around, looking lost, so I took her in.'

'Washington!?' Charles was startled but then remembered that the U.S. border was only about forty kilometres away. 'How did you get my phone number?'

'I called the vet… on the dog's tag… he gave me your number.'

'Is the dog hurt?' Charles was anxious.

'Nah… she's okay.'

'Thank God.' Charles breathed. 'How can I get her back? I haven't got a car.'

'Look, Edmunds, I'm a driver for Mayflower Trucking Company. I got a friend—another driver—who is going up to Kelowna tomorrow and through Penticton. He could bring the dog but he'll have to buy a cage and he wants to be paid something.'

'That's fine,' Charles agreed at once.

'So if you send $300 to me via Western Union at Oroville today, I'll get the dog on her way tomorrow.'

'All right,' Charles was relieved. 'Give me your name again.'

'Ben Volker… V-O-L-K-E-R… and that's $300 American, not Canadian.'

'I'll do it right away.' Charles was excited and happy. 'Where will your friend drop off the dog?'

'At the vet's… I got his address. Look for a yellow and green Mayflower Truck.'

'That's just wonderful! And thanks so much for your time and trouble.'

'No problem.' He hung up.

Charles Edmunds promptly went to his bank to arrange for the transfer of money to Western Union. His spirits lifted on the way home and he had a good sleep for the first time in several nights.

On the following day, Charles waited around the house until early afternoon and then decided to walk to the vet's; it was not a long walk and he would have to go there anyhow to get Penny. Across the street from the vet's office was a small park. Since it was a warm day, he decided to sit on a bench from which he could see the Mayflower truck arrive.

The afternoon dragged on. He watched the birds playing games with a squirrel. A few people paused to chat. No truck arrived. Doubt and worry began to nag at his mind. Shortly before six o'clock, when the vet's office was due to close, Charles went in and spoke to the receptionist. They had had no telephone call about Penny and no one had asked for Edmunds' phone number.

Charles walked slowly home, limping now as pain spread to his leg. His mind was numb. How could anyone be so cruel and unfeeling as to cheat an old man out of money on the pretext of finding a lost pet? He didn't know that such people existed. The walk home was long and despairing. Head down, oblivious to traffic, he neither knew nor cared what happened to him.

Then as he approached the front gate he saw a black bundle of fur lying there. It was Penny! Dirty, begrimed, fur matted, noticeably thinner, her large brown eyes clearly asking forgiveness for being a bad dog. Charles gave her a fierce hug and Penny thumped her long tail in delight. His spirits soared as he opened the gate—the world was coming right again.

Penny ambled into the yard, paused to inspect her rear end, and then searched for any sign of feline intrusion. Charles led her into the house where she inspected her dishes, toy box and teddy bear. Charles watched her lovingly. She was in poor condition and would need a lot of T.L.C. How he looked forward to doing it!

Mama's Boy

Gertrude Parrish sat at her kitchen table, nibbled at her pencil, and agonized over the advertisement that she intended to place in the Vancouver Sun.

She would have to give her age. But she could easily shave off two years because she knew that she looked younger than her years. This would give her 64—just under the universal entry into old age.

She could say that she was lively, in good health (her only time in hospital had been for her gall bladder and that was ten years ago), and liked to play bridge and go to the theatre—all of which was true.

She would have to say that she was a widow. Since her husband, Ben, died five years ago she had been quite lonely and didn't like living by herself. She had tried to find a man by joining the church and the local Seniors Centre where she played bridge every Monday and attended all of their functions, but all of the un-married ones were either too old or too weary.

She knew that she was still attractive—hadn't she won a beauty contest in High School? Of course, she wasn't very tall and a few pounds over-weight, but good clothes could cover most anything. No point in mentioning hair colour since she wore a variety of wigs to cover her sparse grey hair. She tried not to wear her glasses outside of her apartment although she often had to squint.

She didn't like the name 'Gertrude' and often told people to call her 'Giselle' but in this case she decided to use her real name. She liked a drink or two—vodka and tonic—but one didn't put that in an advertisement.

Finally, she completed it:

ATTRACTIVE WIDOW. AGE 64. IN GOOD
HEALTH. ENJOYS BRIDGE, THEATRE

AND MUSIC. WOULD LIKE TO MEET
UNATTACHED MALE ABOUT SAME AGE
WITH SIMILAR INTERESTS. BOX _____

Reviewing the advertisement, Gertrude began to have cold feet. Was this the right thing to do? But how else could she find a man? Would only 'Kooks' reply? Still—it was only a Box Number; nobody would know who she was and if none of the replies (assuming she got any) were suitable, she could drop the whole thing. She reached for the phone.

Gertrude Parrish received three replies. Two of them were 'off the wall' but one was interesting. He gave his name as Cecil Lamont, age 69, un-married, shared her interests and was an expert bridge player. He gave a Box Number for her reply, asking for her phone number so he could contact her (if she was interested) because he was hard to reach by telephone as he still worked part-time.

She thought it rather strange, but wrote a reply giving her phone number and a few more details. Cecil Lamont called a few days later and they arranged to meet for lunch. She was a little nervous as she entered the restaurant, looking for a slim man in a blue jacket, as she had been told. She knew that she looked nice in a black suit with white trim and a new, black wig; not too much make-up and a touch of Chantel. She saw him rise from a table. He was thin and not very tall, about 5'6" she reckoned, with glasses and receding grey hair. Not very imposing! But he was neatly dressed in his blue jacket, grey slacks and a colourful tie.

'Cecil Lamont?' Gertrude enquired, tentatively.

'Yes… and you must be Gertrude.' He stood up and pulled out a chair. 'Do sit down.'

'Thank you.' She sat down, rather at a loss for words. 'It's very warm today, isn't it?'

'Yes, it is. Did you drive here or walk or…?'

'I took a taxi. But I don't live far from here… on 12th Avenue near Granville.'

'Oh, I live around there, too.' As the waiter approached he said, 'would you like a drink before lunch?'

She would have liked a strong vodka but replied, 'Perhaps a glass of white wine.'

'Good,' he nodded to the waiter, 'I'll have the same.'

Conversation was desultory and rather forced as they began to get acquainted. The waiter left menus. Gertrude scanned hers but couldn't read it properly without her glasses, which she didn't have with her.

'What would you like?' Cecil asked.

'Why don't you order for both of us,' she replied, coyly.

He did so. By the end of the meal they were talking more freely. His impression was of a pretty lady, a bit over-weight, rather vain, and looking hard for a man. Her impression was of a rather dry fellow, no forceful personality, well mannered and polite and with a kind, thoughtful demeanor.

They agreed to meet for dinner a few days later. Over this meal, tensions eased and their investigations continued.

'Were you never married?' Gertrude asked.

'No,' Cecil replied, ruefully. 'Never met the right girl, I guess. But you were?'

'Yes... for 46 years. My husband died of cancer five years ago.'

'I'm sorry. Any children?'

'Two—a boy and a girl. They both live in Vancouver but I don't see much of them.'

'Why is that?'

'Oh, I dunno. They seem to live their own lives. Neither of them have children.'

'Were you born around here?'

'No. I was born in Manitoba. My parents came to B.C. during the Great Depression. How about you?'

'I was born in the Fraser Valley—in Ladner.'

'You were an accountant?'

'I still am,' Cecil replied. 'I work part-time for a brokerage company.'

Aided by a bottle of wine, conversation flowed freely and they began to feel comfortable with each other.

After the meal, he asked: 'May I drive you home?'

'Yes... thank you,' Gertrude, who had arrived in a taxi, replied. She was impressed to be escorted to a Lincoln Town Car and had noticed that Cecil had ordered the most expensive dinner and wine on the menu. Obviously, he was not short of money.

As he stopped at her apartment, Gertrude remarked: 'You said that you were a good bridge player. Would you like to partner me at our Senior's Centre next Monday?'

'All right,' he agreed. 'What time shall I pick you up?'

'They start at 7:30.'

'I'll be here at 7:00 o'clock.'

'Thank you!'

Gertrude was delighted at the curiosity and the raised eyebrows of her fellow bridge players when she entered with Cecil Lamont. It quickly became apparent that he was an expert. He always arrived at the right contract and arranged so that he played the hand. Although she was just an average player, they quickly gathered points and, at the end of the evening, were awarded the prize for first place.

Driving home, Gertrude was glowing. 'Where did you learn to play bridge like that?'

'It was a hobby at one time,' he replied. 'I played a lot of Duplicate and have a few Master Points but I haven't played much recently.'

'Well, you haven't lost your touch.'

'Thanks… I enjoyed it… let's do it again.'

He pulled the car up in front of her apartment building.

'Would you like to come up for a cup of coffee?' asked Gertrude, who had something else in mind.

'I don't think so, thanks. I have to work tomorrow morning.'

'Oh.' She was clearly disappointed. 'When will I see you again?'

'How about dinner later on in the week? I'll give you a call.'

'All right.' She leaned across the car and kissed his cheek. 'Good night.'

'Good night.'

Gertrude was a bit frustrated at Cecil's lack of initiative but mollified the next day to receive a dozen roses and an invitation to dinner on the following Friday. After the dinner, which included drinks before, wine with, and liqueurs after, Cecil accepted her invitation 'for coffee'. No coffee was drunk but after a vodka they headed for the bedroom. Since neither of them had had sex for some time, their love making was tentative and, as far as Gertrude was concerned, over too soon.

She snuggled up to him. 'My, that was nice.' Not brilliant, she thought, but better than nothing.

'Yes, it was,' he agreed, stroking her back.

'I have a little confession to make,' she said, archly. 'I'm not 64 years old… I'm 66.'

'That's all right,' he replied, drily. 'I'm not 69… I'm 71.'

'Oh, you…' she giggled. She began to stroke him, trying for an arousal.

Instead, he disentangled himself, got out of bed and began to get dressed. 'I'll have to be going now. I have to work tomorrow.'

'Do you really have to go?' Gertrude was very frustrated.

'Yes, I do.' He finished dressing and headed for the bedroom door. 'I'll see you on Monday.'

Thus, it became an established routine. Bridge on Monday. Dinner on Friday, followed by sex. As time went on, Cecil became a bit more proficient at the act and Gertrude had an orgasm occasionally. But there was little after-play. He would not spend the night and when she suggested a week-end away together, he dismissed the idea summarily. It began to dawn on Gertrude that she knew very little about him. She had never been to his apartment and wasn't even sure exactly where he lived. She didn't know his phone number, although it was probably in the book, because he always called her. He was not short of money since he drove a Lincoln and spent freely. She vowed to remedy this situation.

They were in bed on the following Friday night, in a mellow mood after making love, when Gertrude broached the subject. 'Do you know, Cecil, that I've never been to your place?'

'H…m…m…,' he mused.

'Next week, after dinner, let's go to your apartment.'

'Ah…' he demurred, 'it wouldn't be convenient.'

'Why not?'

'Well… Ah… you see… I don't live alone.'

Gertrude sat bolt upright in bed, the sheet dropping from her bare shoulders. Adrenaline surged through her body. What did he mean? Had he lied when he said that he wasn't married? Did he live common-law? Was he gay?

'With whom do you live?' she demanded.

'My mother.'

'Your mother!' There was something weird about a 71-year old man living with his mother. 'How old is she?'

'Ninety-three.'

'Good grief! How long have you been living with her?'

'Since my father died.'

'When was that?'

'In 1960!'

'Do you mean,' Gertrude was astounded, 'that you have been living with your mother for 41 years?'

'Yes.'

'Have you never wanted a family of your own… a wife and kids?'

'I've thought about it from time to time but it never seemed convenient. It's my duty to look after my mother. I owe her a lot. I'm an only child and she took good care of me. Now it's my turn to take care of her.'

'But she must need a lot of care,' Gertrude said. 'How is her health?'

'Not too good. Her memory is almost gone. She needs a wheel chair to get around.'

'Why don't you put her in a nursing home?'

'I couldn't bear to see her in one of those places. She would die right away.'

Gertrude thought that his mother, at age 93, was probably ready to go anyway, but didn't say so. 'Do you do all the housework, make the meals and everything?'

'Yes. And I can't leave her alone for very long.'

Well, Gertrude thought, that explained a few things. 'Do you have some help?'

'Yes. A nurse comes in twice a week and the lady next door sits with her at times.'

Gertrude sighed. 'She is ruining your life.'

'It's not like that,' Cecil said sharply. 'I can still do the things I want.'

'Oh, sure,' she responded, sarcastically. 'I wanted us to go to

Hawaii for a week but I suppose there is no point in suggesting that?'

'I'm afraid not.' He got out of bed and began to put on his clothes.

Gertrude flopped back on the bed. 'Are you gonna introduce me to your mother?'

'I don't think it would be wise.'

'But she knows about me?'

'She knows I'm seeing someone—yes.'

'And she doesn't like it?'

'She has never said that.'

'Just implied it, eh?'

Cecil didn't answer the question but just finished dressing. 'I'd better go now.'

'Yeah,' Gertrude said wearily, 'Go and tend to Mama.'

Over the ensuing weeks Gertrude found the problem of Cecil's mother constantly gnawing at her mind. It was obvious that, every time he went out, Cecil told his mother what time he would return. As that time approached, no matter what they were doing, even making love, he began to fidget and look surreptitiously at his watch. He would never make a commitment in advance, obviously having to check with his mother beforehand and they never deviated from their twice-weekly meetings. Gertrude pictured him giving his mother a bath and lifting her on and off the toilet and was revolted at the thought. She began to hate the woman that she had never met.

The inevitable happened. One evening, just after returning to her apartment after dinner, Gertrude said that she had two tickets for the Vancouver Symphony on the following evening. Would Cecil go with her?

'Ah…' he stalled. 'It's rather short notice.'

'Do you have something else on?' she asked.

'No,' he admitted. 'It's just that we usually have some food sent in and get a video on Saturday nights.'

'You could change your plans for once.'

'Well… I don't know…'

Gertrude lost her temper. 'What's the matter, Thethil?' she lisped. 'Won't Mama let you go out?'

'It's not that...' he started.

But Gertrude was rolling. 'I'm sick of this routine... bridge on Monday... screw on Friday... we never do anything else. Every time I suggest anything else you say 'No' because you have to check with Mama. And we both know what Mama will say, don't we?'

'She doesn't...' he started again.

She interrupted. 'You'll never be a man. You're tied to Mama's apron strings and always will be.' Her voice rose in pitch. 'No wonder you never got married... you're married already... to Mama!'

'I'll try...'

'Don't bother,' she stormed. 'just get out! I don't want to ever see you again. Go home to Mama. You're a lousy lover anyway.'

Cecil Lamont blanched and left without another word.

'To hell with him.' Gertrude said to herself. 'I'll find a real man. Maybe I'll change that advertisement slightly the next time.'

Douglas Finstead

Helen Finstead poked her husband in the back, trying to get him to roll over before his snoring rattled the pictures off the wall. It woke him up.

'Ah… hey… what's going on?' Douglas mumbled, sleepily.

'You're snoring again.' She sat up in bed. 'Lord… you'll wake up the whole neighborhood.'

'You woke me up just to tell me that?'

'Well, you're keeping me awake. You might as well be awake, too.'

'What time is it?' He looked at his bedside clock. 'God… five-thirty… I have to get up for work at seven.'

'It's not my fault,' Helen said, sharply. 'You've had the problem for the 29 years that we've been married and done nothing about it.'

Wide awake now, Douglas Finstead abandoned any hope of further sleep that night. 'It's not that bad.'

'How do you know?' she demanded. 'You can't hear it.'

'You could wear ear plugs,' he suggested, weakly.

'I tried that. They are too uncomfortable and I don't feel secure not being able to hear anything. Suppose there was trouble…'

It now being six o'clock, Douglas got out of bed saying: 'Come on, let's get up and have some breakfast!' He pulled a dressing gown over his spare frame; he was a thin man in spite of little exercise.

The breakfast nook in the house, in the Vancouver district of Kerrisdale, faced east and on this warm July day the sunrise gave promise of a fine day. 'See,' he gestured, 'it's nice to watch the sun come up.'

'Yeah.' Helen was not impressed with nature's bounty. She wore a ratty dressing gown and her grey hair was un-combed. She looked older than her 63 years but was in good health apart from her teeth which were poor and which she refused to have taken out.

Hoping to lighten her mood, Douglas suggested: 'Why don't you come into town for lunch today?'

'It's too much trouble to take the bus,' she replied. They had only one car.

'It's only fifteen minutes.' For the past 12 years Douglas had worked as a claims adjuster for B.C. Insurance Corporation. 'We could try that new Romeo's.'

'No. I want to do some gardening today and I won't have enough energy to do both.' She paused. 'Especially after that lousy night's sleep.'

'I'm sorry.' He was not an inconsiderate man but he seemed unable to come to grips with the problem that was so annoying to his wife and had also been to his son, Carl, when he had lived at home. He was always tired. He was not aware that his fellow employees at B.C.I.C. called him 'Dagwood Bumstead' because of his habit of dozing off at his desk; although he was puzzled to hear his boss come into the office that Douglas shared with several others and ask: 'Where's Bumstead?' and then proceed to his own desk. (His boss would likely have made an issue of Finstead's tiredness had he not had just a year to go before the mandatory retirement age of 65.)

'For a while,' Helen interrupted his thoughts, 'your snoring was better but now it's worse than ever. I want you to go to an eye-ear-nose specialist.'

'I dunno…'

'You know it's bad. On our holiday last month the people in the next room in the motel hammered on the wall because you were keeping them awake.'

'Yeah… well…'

'As soon as you come in from work,' Helen plowed on, 'you have a nap. What if you fell asleep driving home in the car?'

'Oh, that won't happen.'

'I don't want to move into the spare bedroom. I like sleeping with you.' Her sex life was far from over. 'But I'll have to if this keeps up.'

'Yeah… well…'

'Well—what?'

'I'll try to find someone,' he sighed. 'I'll make some enquiries at work.'

Working in the garden, Helen regretted that she had not accepted the invitation for lunch. They had very little social life. Douglas was older than most of his fellow workers and she was self-conscious about her bad teeth. Their only child, Carl, lived in West Vancouver, married but without children, and they saw him only infrequently. She would have liked more children but a miscarriage ended that hope. She would have liked a part-time job but there was no chance of that. She sighed. Perhaps they could do some travelling after he retired next year. She wondered if modern women ever had this problem; sleeping together before marriage as they did now would surely show it up.

Being a natural procrastinator, Douglas found a myriad of excuses to avoid going to a doctor. But the problem nagged at his mind. He remembered growing up in Regina when family holidays were spent touring the country in a large trailer; he was always relegated to a pup tent outside because his snoring in a confined space was, his father said: 'Like two chipmunks inside a kettle drum.'

He recalled the problem occurring after the family moved to Vancouver (he was 16 years old) when he fell asleep in school. The Principal sent a note home. His father told him to: 'Make sure you stay in a crowd so that if you go to sleep, you won't fall over.'

Completing an accountancy course after High School, Douglas found a job with a large auditing firm which was where he met Helen, who also worked there. They married in 1965. He wondered if that firm had let him go, after 32 years, because of his propensity to fall asleep. Certainly, Helen began to complain of his snoring almost immediately after they were married.

Douglas did try to alleviate the problem. He had his tonsils out—no help. He left his dentures out at night—no change. He inhaled before bedtime to clear his passages—no effect. He tried to stay awake until Helen had gone to sleep but he was usually too tired to do so.

Then for a while, the snoring eased off and they both thought that the problem had gone away. Not so—it was now back at full blast.

All of these thoughts flowed through his mind as Douglas procrastinated. Eventually, however, he ran out of excuses and had to make an appointment with a specialist. Helen spent that day like a 'Nervous Nellie', finding meaningless household jobs that didn't need doing. As soon as Douglas came in the door, she asked, impatiently: 'Well... what happened?'

'For Heaven's sake!' he protested, 'let me take off my jacket and get a beer.'

They sat down at the kitchen table. 'I prob'ly have 'Apnea',' he said, 'it's a Greek word... 'a' means 'not' and 'pnea' means 'breath'.

'Very interesting,' Helen remarked, drily, 'but what do you have to do about it?'

'I have to go into the hospital over-night for some tests.'

'What kind of tests?'

'I dunno... they take a video of my eye balls while I'm asleep and some other stuff.'

'Oh.' Helen was disappointed. 'When do you have to go in?'

'Tonight.' I have to be there by nine o'clock.'

'But surely the doctor said what might be causing the snoring?'

'Yeah... blocked passages. But he wouldn't say what might or might not have to be done, pending the outcome of the tests. These damn doctors! They'll never commit themselves... perhaps this... maybe that...'

So Douglas spent the night in the hospital and when he came home the next morning, he was exhausted.

'Coffee!' he demanded, as he sank into a kitchen chair.

'What happened?' Helen asked, as she poured him a cup.

'You've never seen anything like it! I had so many wires and tubes attached it was like getting the Space Shuttle ready for launch.'

'To record what?'

'Brain waves, tongue twitches, leg jerks, eye movements, oxygen saturation, carbon dioxide level...'

'Good Grief!'

'I apparently have 'Sleep Apnea'. That means that the back of my throat becomes constricted when I'm asleep.'

'And...?'

'So I try to breathe, can't... wake up for a moment and then fall asleep again. I never get a proper sleep called R.E.M.—Rapid Eye Movement—which the body has to have.'

'What does that mean—R.E.M.?'

'Apparently, during R.E.M. sleep the eye pupils dart around under the eyelids as they watch the real-life dream images being projected out of the subconscious mind and this is essential for proper rest.'

'Which is why you're always tired during the day?'

'Right. The Doc said I could even fall asleep while driving a car.'

'I told you so!' Helen said, triumphantly. 'So, what is the cure?'

'The only cure is a thing called a Continuous Positive Airway Pressure machine. You have to wear a mask at night; air is forced through your nose to keep the nasal passages clear.'

'Where do you get this device?'

'He's getting me one tomorrow.'

'H...m...m...,' Helen was doubtful. She was rightly so.

Douglas sat in his chair in the living room to demonstrate the C.P.A.P. 'The mask fits over your face like this and you adjust the strap around your head for a snug fit.' Which he did. 'The hose goes to this Control Unit which has a small blower motor to push the air into your nose. I'll set it at medium flow.'

Sitting back in his chair, he could feel the air flowing into his nose. 'Seems to be okay... we'll see how it goes tonight.'

Douglas settled himself into bed, laying on his back, and adjusted the mask and the strap; the Control Unit was on a bed-side table. It felt very strange. He relaxed and concentrated his thoughts on pleasant things, which was his normal procedure when going to sleep. He usually slept on his right side. So he turned over. The mask slipped out of place. He mumbled and set it right. How was he ever going to get to sleep with this contraption on? He flipped his pillow over to the cool side.

Next to him, Helen was aware of his discomfort.

Douglas dozed off. In the middle of the night he woke up and decided to have a drink of water from his bed-side glass. Forgetting that he had the mask on, he poured the water over it, his chest and his pajamas. Cursing, he got out of bed, dried the mask and changed pajamas.

By this time, Helen was wide awake.

It was a long night for them both. Doze... wake up... doze again.

On the next night, being very tired, Douglas went straight to sleep. Then Helen was shocked into wakefulness by a violent jerk as Douglas tore off the mask and shouted: 'I'm being strangled!' He had rolled over in his sleep and the hose had curled around his throat; his subconscious obviously told him that he was being strangled to death.

'XOXO,' he swore. 'That's enough of this stupid thing for to-night.

'Yes,' Helen soothed. 'Turn it off for tonight.'

'I sure will.' Douglas tucked himself in, quickly went to sleep... and snored.

Helen swore.

On the following night, she urged him to try again. 'Don't give up too soon. After all, you paid $400.00 for this machine.'

'Yeah... all right.'

It was three o'clock in the morning when an almighty crash jolted them both awake. Douglas had rolled over, probably more than once, and the hose had pulled the Control Unit off the bed-side table on to the floor, carrying with it a glass of water and the clock.

'I hope to hell it's broken,' Douglas snarled, while they sorted themselves out.

'It seems to be okay,' Helen said, helping to set things back in place.

'Too bad,' he mumbled, as he put the mask back on.

But gradually Douglas grew accustomed to the C.P.A.P., learning how to get settled and move carefully. The results were evident immediately. He no longer felt tired during the day and became aware of how his life had been limited by the lack of proper R.E.M. sleep. His colleagues at work no longer called him 'Dagwood Bumstead'.

Helen, too, was less tired and more healthy. She almost forgot the time when she had the urge to put a pillow over his face... and try not to leave it there for too long.

Granpa Bert and the Train

Wayne Quenten was six years old and been in school now for three months. He was not too well adjusted. He was fine academically and had no trouble with his studies. The problem was social—he often knew what the teacher and the other pupils were going to say before they said it. And he always knew when some one was lying.

One day the teacher—a young lady of 27—asked one of the boys: 'What does your father do for a living?'

'He is an architect,' the boy replied, proudly.

Wayne knew this was a lie; the man was a draughtsman for a contractor but had failed his architectural course.

'But…' Wayne started to correct the boy but then stopped.

'You were going to say something, Wayne?' the teacher asked.

'No,' Wayne replied. He realised that he would be laughed at; how could he know about that? As a result, he was shy and spoke only when spoken to. He realised that he was different from the other kids and possessed an ability that seemed to be unique to him. It was worrisome.

Two years earlier, at the age of four, he had spent a weekend with his aunt Clara while his parents had a short holiday. In her garden he spoke to a small boy, about his own age, with curly black hair and big brown eyes, whose name was Ross.

'Why does Ross not come into the house?' he asked his aunt.

Clara's eyes bulged from her head in consternation. Ross was the name of her son who had died, at age five, many years ago. 'Ross is dead, dear,' she said.

'No, he isn't,' Wayne said, firmly. 'He talks to me.'

Clara of course reported the incident to Wayne's mother, Ilena, saying; 'Do you think he really saw Ross?'

'Maybe,' Ilena replied. 'Wayne is different.'

She had seen her son do some strange things. One day, entering the dining room, she found Wayne standing in front of four chairs, speaking in turn to each one. The chairs of course were empty.

'What are you doing, dear?' she asked.

'We're having a quiz,' he replied.

'Who are your friends?'

'They are just pretend,' he said quickly. Although they really weren't—he knew the name of each one.

'Well,' Ilena said, 'it's time for lunch so send them away now.'

'All right.'

The Quenten family lived in a large house in the Kerrisdale district of Vancouver. They were four. Wayne's father, Stuart, was a lawyer with a large down town firm. His wife, Ilena, was a social worker. Stuart's father lived with them in a lower level suite that had been re-modelled to provide a bedroom, bath and a large living area. He had been with them for three years, since his wife, Constance, had died. His name was Bertram, always called 'Bert'. He was 72 years old and in poor health following a four-way, by-pass, heart operation two years ago.

After his heart operation Granpa Bert, needing a sedentary occupation, decided to build a model railway for his grandson. The project soon took on a life of its own and now virtually filled all of his time and all of his living room. Fifty feet of track went past three stations, over two bridges, through a tunnel and even disappeared behind a wall for two feet. The eight driving wheels of an E.M.D. F-9 engine pulled a variety of coaches—pullmans, dining cars, baggage cars and an observation car. Behind one station was a model town with stores, houses and a church. Behind another was a mountain.

It was Wayne's habit to come home from school, grab a glass of milk and two chocolate chip cookies, and go down stairs to see what Granpa Bert was doing. His mother, Ilena, worked staggered hours and tried to be at home when Wayne arrived but it was not always possible. On this day she was not at home as Wayne went down stairs. 'Hi, Granpa Bert... what are you doing?'

Bert looked up. 'Hello, Wayne... I'm fixing this connection'. He was a frail man, thin, whispy grey hair, glasses. A civil engineer, he was quite clever mechanically. 'If you will hold these ends together,' Bert pointed, 'I will solder them.'

Wayne did as ordered but Bert's hand, holding the soldering iron, shook so much that it was a poor join.

After 45 minutes of working and playing on the railroad Wayne said: 'I just heard Mom come in… I'll go and see what's for dinner.'

'All right, son,' Bert said, heavily.

As Wayne turned to go he saw a black aura above Granpa Bert's head.

In the kitchen he found his mother making dinner preparations. 'Mom,' he said, 'Granpa Bert is going to die.'

Ilena turned to face him. 'We all die sooner or later.'

'No… I mean quite soon.'

'How do you know?'

'I can feel it.'

Ilena had seen evidence of Wayne's E.S.P. and knew that he was psychic. Trying to understand, so that she could help him, Ilena had read widely on the subject. She now knew that everyone is psychic to some degree, from simple cases of 'Deja vu' to the remarkable psychics.

The 'Sleeping Prophet'—Edgar Cayce—with no medical training had diagnosed hundreds of cases of illness in people whom he never met and prescribed treatment, often with herbal remedies that the doctors had never heard of. Fortunately, his family kept meticulous records and followed up to ensure that Cayce's remedies worked, as they almost always did. Maybe Wayne would be able to do that!

It seemed that Wayne could get in touch with people on the 'Other Side', like such famous psychics as Eileen Garrett and Arthur Ford, and reveal facts not known to anyone living. It was Arthur Ford who became famous for the 'Houdini Affair'. For most of his life Houdini took great pleasure in debunking phoney mediums— and there were many of them! But as he grew older he began to realise that some people were providing true information, not known to people. So Houdini devised a coded message, known only to his wife and himself; whoever died first was to try to get the message through. Houdini himself died first and passed the message to Arthur Ford, who knew neither of the Houdinis. His wife confirmed that the message was correct.

After reading those books and others by Raymond Moody and George Anderson, Ilena knew that life after death was a reality. She agreed with one writer who said: 'There is now so much proof of life after death that anyone who does not believe can no longer be called a skeptic—he is merely ignorant'.

One evening when Wayne was about to go to bed, he asked his mother: 'What happens when you die?'

'Your body is buried, or cremated, and your soul goes to heaven.'

'What is a soul?'

Ilena searched for words. 'It is like a spiritual part of you.'

'But you can't see it?'

'No.'

'Then when your soul goes to heaven, does it become your body again?'

'Yes.'

'Suppose you are old and sick like Granpa Bert and don't want to be in that body?'

Ilena had to improvise. 'I think that you can be any age you wish to be.'

'Oh.' Wayne thought about that for a minute. 'Do people come back to earth?'

'You mean, like ghosts?'

'No,' Wayne said, impatiently. 'I know all about Play People… I mean real people.'

'I'm not sure,' Ilena replied. She had read Dr. Ian Stevenson's book: 'Twenty Cases Suggestive of Reincarnation' and had to admit that his research was impeccable and that several cases were very realistic. But she still was not fully convinced. 'I think so, but we will have to leave that question until you are older.'

'Thank you.' Wayne gave his mother a hug and went to bed.

Two days later Granpa Bert died of a massive heart attack. Wayne was allowed to come to the funeral and felt very sad at the loss of his old friend.

Shortly after the funeral, Wayne came home one day after school. His mother was not home but he had a key in case of this event. Grabbing his usual glass of milk and two chocolate chip cookies, he went down stairs to the railway. As soon as he sat down in front of the control panel, he felt Granpa Bert's presence. For several minutes Wayne just looked at the railway and did nothing but eat his cookies and drink his milk. He kept his hands folded in his lap. Then, with sudden inspiration, he said: 'Power On.'

The Power Switch flipped to 'On'.

'Speed 10 mph,' Wayne ordered.

The rotary dial controlling the speed moved to 10 mph, and the train pulled away from the first station.

Wayne gave a beaming smile. He and Granpa Bert were going to have some great fun!

The Devil's Television

Most visitors to The City are not aware that there is a large Fair Ground which has games, rides and side-shows and which is open the year around. Once a year, for two weeks in the Fall, it expands. Additional games and side-shows arrive, contests are held for best produce and animals and the Fair calls itself an Exhibition. For the other 50 weeks of the years the Fair attracts a small but steady flow of customers and provides jobs for many people. Those who work there year around are a representative cross-section of society; some are kind, caring and generous; some are cruel, dishonest and venal. They are a close, self-contained community who stick together and help each other out in time of trouble.

Irene (call me Renee) Fox had spent all of her working life at the Fair; she was now 35 years old. Coming straight from High School, she had known no other life. Her family had lived nearby and the carnival atmosphere attracted her; she loved the constantly-changing scene. Pretty, naive and vulnerable at the age of 18, she was easy prey for a smooth-talking shill named Bert Fox who bedded her quickly and only reluctantly married her a year later when she became pregnant.

The result was her son, Shawn, now 16 years old. But Bert was long gone; unwilling to be tied down he had disappeared shortly after the baby's birth and Irene had not seen him since. She had not bothered to file for divorce, nor to revert to her maiden name, which was Davis.

In addition to Shawn, Bert had left her with another problem, an addiction to alcohol, which was evident by the network of thin, red veins on her face. But her dark hair had no grey and she didn't need glasses. She was extroverted and vivacious and had no trouble in attracting customers to what ever facility she was working on at the time.

Irene had held a variety of jobs—bingo caller, barker, candy floss seller—and now sold tickets and operated the Bumper Car Ride. But at this moment the B.C.R. was not operating—to the annoyance of many young riders already in the cars. Her common-law husband, Phil Olsen, who was an electrician, was busy at a nearby terminal box trying to correct the fault.

'How much longer, Phil?' Irene asked, rubbing her forehead in a vain attempt to ease her hangover.

'Not long now.' He didn't look up. Phil was 50 years old, heavily built with a generous paunch from drinking. His dark hair was getting sparse and grey at the temples. He was a stolid, phlegmatic fellow with little imagination. However, he was good at his job and had once held a well-paying position with Hydro which he had lost due to alcohol. 'I just have to clean up this corroded connection and you should be okay.'

Irene grimaced as the power was restored and the bumper cars started up, their young riders shouting and screaming. Not great for a hangover but what else was new. A couple of vodkas at lunch time would set the world right again.

'There you go,' Phil said, as he packed up his carry-all.

'Gee, thanks,' Irene said, listlessly. 'Where are you going now?'

'To the Ferris Wheel.'

'See you later.'

'Will you be home for dinner as usual… about six o'clock?'

'Yeah… if I live that long. Why?'

'I've got a surprise for you.'

'What is it?'

'I'll tell you at home.' Phil strolled away.

Shawn Fox did not bother to go to school that afternoon, spending the time in a video parlour with some pals. He had just started grade ten, having barely scraped through grade nine, and was not interested in anything scholastic. His interests were, in priority, gambling, girls, drinking, pot and cars. Unfortunately, in his opinion, he didn't have enough money to satisfy all of his needs. His mother had found him a week-end job at the Fair but that money was invariably gone by Tuesday. He had started to look for a full-time job so that he could quit school and find his own pad. Meanwhile, he was forced to live in a dingy apartment with his mother and Phil Olsen who spent all their time drinking and didn't give a shit about him.

Shawn Fox was blessed with charisma. He was tall and slim with black, curly hair, a charming smile and frank blue eyes that radiated innocence. He was also almost amoral. He had no hesitation in lying, cheating or stealing to get his own way. His clever, devious behaviour had earned him the nickname 'Foxy' from his mates. Irene and Phil had learned never to leave money or other valuables within Shawn's reach. That he had not yet been picked up by the police was pure luck. He also had a violent temper.

Governments across Canada, at all levels, are hooked on gambling; the temptation of easy money is too great. Gambling is estimated to be a $20 Billion a year industry, where there are a plethora of lotteries, slots and casinos in every Province. And the future looks stupendous! Just imagine an 'Online Casino'—thousands of simultaneous players, no hotel to run, no staff to pay, no machines to buy—all profit!

Of course there is a social cost. It is addictive. Many cannot really afford to do so and gamble with rent money, grocery budget or stolen money. This takes a terrible toll on family and friends. There are probably one million people in Canada with gambling problems. There are awareness campaigns, prevention and treatment programs. These include hotlines, training professionals who already work with drug and alcohol addicts and school education programs. One way to pay for all this is to open another Casino!

Although the Province had a yearly revenue of $1.5 Billion, it looked enviously at Ontario who was raking in $3.0 Billion from its various schemes and was coining money from the new Video Lottery Terminals. The VLTs brought in as much money as all the other machines combined.

The temptation was too great. The political party in power granted permission for both destination casinos and for VLTs. They completely ignored the fact that, while they were in Opposition, they had vociferously objected to gambling in all its forms. Greed is insatiable.

Video Lottery Terminals are so addictive to young people that they are known as 'The Devil's Television'. They are the 'Crack cocaine of gambling'. A study by the University of Windsor on close to 1,000 teen-agers showed that five percent of them were already problem gamblers and another 9.4% at high risk. Nevertheless, the Province licenced VLTs in neighborhood stores, malls and video halls. One of their first addicts was Shawn Fox.

Phil, Irene and Shawn all arrived at home at about the same time that day. Home was a two-bedroom apartment in an elderly building, furnished by Phil in K-Mart motif. The adults settled down to have drinks. Shawn asked: 'What's for dinner?'

Irene replied. 'There's some Kentucky Fried Chicken in the fridge... stick it in the microwave.'

'Do you want some?'

'Not right now.' Drinks came first.

Shawn had a quick meal and left, saying: 'I'm going out.'

'Where to?' Irene asked.

'Just around with the guys.'

'What about homework?'

'Don't have any.'

'Well... don't be too late.'

'I won't.' The door closed behind him.

Irene sighed and poured another drink of vodka. 'I wonder what he gets up to?'

'Boys will be boys,' Phil remarked, who couldn't care less what Shawn did.

'Hey!' Irene shouted, remembering. 'What's the surprise you have for me?'

Phil took a swallow of beer and grinned. 'How would you like to go on a six-month cruise on a luxury liner?'

'Oh, sure,' Irene scoffed. 'And win a million dollars on the lottery.'

'No... I'm serious. Remember Fred Kessler?'

'Who used to work with you... sure.'

'Well... he had this job as electrician on the cruise ship all lined up and he broke his leg. I can have the job if I want it.'

'What about your job at the Fair Grounds?'

'I'm not under contract; they just call me when they need me.'

Irene's eyes sparkled. 'And I can go along?'

'Yeah... there's a double cabin and you get treated just like a passenger.'

'Whoopee!' Irene shouted. 'When does it go and where to?'

'Next month from here, through the Panama Canal, tour the Caribbean and back home in April.'

'Wonderful! Take it... take it!'

'Okay. But what about Shawn?'

Irene paused to think. 'Maybe my mother will take him in.'

'In that small apartment?'

'It's got a den that Shawn could have... it's big enough for a bed and a chest of drawers.'

'I don't know...' Phil started.

'I'll call my mother tomorrow,' Irene said, firmly.

Norma Davis did not see a great deal of her daughter and was a bit surprised when Irene asked herself over in the evening but of course said 'Yes.' Norma had a small, basement apartment not too far from Phil's. The windows were at ground level. She had bought it in 1985 when her husband died. It had a kitchen with barely enough room for a table and two chairs. A little den by the front door was used for storage. The bedroom had a double bed, chest of drawers, cedar chest, two chairs and pictures on the walls of her late husband, Irene and Bert and Shawn. In the living room was a chesterfield, two arm chairs, TV, coffee table and three occasional chairs. On the walls were prints of the harbour and of the Rocky Mountains. Between the living room and the kitchen was an open divider on which was displayed Norma's glass collection. This was her pride and joy, amassed over many years—jars, jugs, bottles, rose stems and other ornaments of varying size and colour. Some were cut glass. When the sun caught them they reflected all the colours of the rainbow. She dusted them lovingly twice a week.

'Come in... come in,' Norma said, opening the door to Irene's knock.

Irene gave her mother a peck on the cheek. 'You're looking pretty good for 80 years old.'

'I'm feeling good right now except for the arthritis. I'll just put the kettle on for a cup of tea.'

'Fine,' Irene said, who would have preferred a stiff rye. After chatting for a while over the tea, she broached the subject of her visit, ending with: '… and would you take Shawn in?'

Norma's face grew somber. 'Oh, I don't know if I could…'

Irene interrupted. 'It's only for six months. Shawn's school is not far from here.'

'But I don't have any room.'

'That little den is just full of stuff that could go in your locker. I'll clear it out for you and put in a bed and a chest of drawers for Shawn. He won't be any trouble.'

'Can't he stay in your apartment?'

'No. Phil just rents it and he doesn't like it much anyway; he's going to give it up.'

'Well…' Norma demurred.

'Of course, I'll leave you some money for his room and board. Really, Shawn spends so little time at home… please, Mother… here's the chance of a lifetime for me.'

'Oh, all right,' Norma gave in.

'Thanks, Mum.' Irene gave her mother a hug. 'I'll come over on the week-end and sort things out.'

The first ten days of Shawn's visit to his grandmother's suite went by quickly. He never did any homework and just came in for a meal and went out again. Norma gave him a door key and he always came in after she was in bed. They had a brief time together in the mornings over breakfast and at the week-end. He still had his job at the Fair Grounds.

Norma did not know that Shawn was spending all his time and money gambling at a Video Lottery Terminal in a local arcade. The appeal of playing poker on a VLT lies in the speed at which one can play, controlled by the player. An adept can complete a game cycle in about $1^1/_2$ seconds which gives the feeling that one is constantly in action and payout is immediate (if one wins!). Shawn couldn't get enough—hour after hour—winning some and losing more—

positive that the big payout was just ahead.

Then, while preparing to go to the store one day, Norma counted her money to find it $20.00 short. She was quite sure of her calculations and confronted Shawn at dinner time. 'Did you borrow $20.00 from my handbag, Shawn?'

'Me? Of course not,' Shawn lied, his blue eyes radiating innocence.

'But I know I had it.'

'Granny... you probably dropped it at the store the last time you were out.'

'No... no... I'm sure I had it at the Seniors Centre yesterday.'

'You must have counted wrong.'

'I guess so.' But Norma was not convinced.

'How are you off for money, anyway?' Shawn asked, casually.

'Well, I just have my O.A.P. plus the supplement.'

'No savings from the sale of the house?'

'Oh, yes... there's some left.'

'Good,' Shawn remarked, as he left for his evening of gambling.

From then on Norma kept a close eye on her handbag and put the money that Irene had given her (which she thought a bit skimpy) for Shawn's board and allowance in the bank.

Shawn rarely went to school in the afternoon and his teacher had nobody to contact about it. He spent the afternoons gambling. In addition to the V.L.T., he needed money for pot and for the running poker game with his cronies. He was desperate for money. A week or so after the purse incident, he stood by the divider in his grandmother's suite and said: 'Gran... can you let me have $50.00?'

'But you just had your allowance,' she demurred.

'Yeah, but I have some heavy expenses at school—books and stuff, y'know.'

'I can't spare any money,' Norma said, firmly.

'I think you can.' Shawn's eyes narrowed and his face grew dark. He took a fragile, blue glass jar with a curved handle from the divider and held it out between thumb and forefinger. 'Be a shame if all your nice glass got broken, wouldn't it?'

'Shawn, don't...'

Shawn dropped it. The jar shattered into a hundred pieces.

'Oh, God,' Norma moaned.

Shawn picked up a rose stem and held it out; 'Fifty bucks, Gran.'

'Yes, yes... all right... don't break any more,' She wiped a tear from her eyes. 'I'll get it for you.'

When the boy left, Norma sank piteously into her chair. What should she do? She supposed that she should call Child Welfare or somebody; but he was her grandson and she did love him and didn't want to see him in trouble with the authorities.

She decided not to have any amount of money in the apartment. When she went shopping, she would go to the bank first and get out the money required and no more. That way, she would never have any money for Shawn to extort.

This worked for a while. Shawn threatened her again with the glass collection but she never had more than ten dollars. Worse was to come.

Spending so many hours in the Video Parlour, Shawn was in the company of several unsavory characters around his own age. They all needed money. He and another boy, age 15, broke into a house and stole the TV and the Stereo; but they got little money from the Fence and it was very risky having no car and having to carry the stolen items down the street. Shawn was smart enough not to repeat that. He vowed only to steal cash in the future. He had borrowed money from the owner of the Video Hall and could not pay it back—the 'Vig' was heavy.

Usually, Norma only saw Shawn at breakfast and at dinner; he was out of the suite all other times and came home after she had gone to bed. This November day, however, Shawn strolled in at lunch time. 'Hi, Gran,' he said casually.

'Shawn!' she was surprised. 'Why are you here? Do you want some lunch?'

'No lunch. I just want to have a chat.'

'What about?' Norma asked, warily.

'Money,' he replied. 'I need some.'

'Now Shawn... you know I don't keep much money here.'

'Yeah... but you got some in the bank, don't you?'

'Well...' her voice wavered.

'Then we'll just have to take a stroll to the bank, won't we?'

'I'm not...' Norma started.

'Yes, you are.' Shawn's back-handed blow caught her across the forehead, spilling her to the chesterfield and sending her glasses across the room.

'Shawn...' she wept, her body trembling.

'Now, now Gran... it's all right,' he found her glasses and helped her to her feet. He said kindly: 'We don't want that to happen again, do we?'

'No,' Norma moaned.

'So just get your cheque book and we'll toddle along to the bank... $500.00 will do for now.'

From that day, Norma's life was terror. She trembled and shook every time she saw her grandson and was afraid to say anything that could be misconstrued. A raised fist by Shawn was enough to send her reeling. In the weeks before Xmas, Shawn had extorted $2,000 from her. She knew that she should call the authorities but Shawn had threatened to kill her if she did; she knew that he might. She would somehow have to survive until Irene returned.

A week prior to Xmas, Shawn was after her again. 'Y'know, Gran... I have to buy Xmas presents and stuff.'

For some unknown reason, Norma, whose bank account now had little left in it, stood firm and said, 'No, Shawn... no more money.'

He clenched his fist in her face. 'You want another beating?'

Norma trembled but would not submit. 'No... there's no money left anyhow.'

'Yes there is... I saw your bank book.'

'Anyhow... no.'

'No what?'

'No more money.'

His blow hit her squarely in the face, breaking her nose and one of her dentures. She fell, moaning, to the floor. Blood poured down her chin. Shawn's face was a mask of fury as his temper raged out of control. He began to kick her 'Take that... and that... you'll give me money or I'll kill you.'

Shawn would probably have killed her had not the door to the suite burst open to admit two policemen. They had been called to the building for another reason and one of them happened to glance in the window to witness the beating. One quickly put the cuffs on Shawn and shouted to his partner to: 'Call 911 for an ambulance.'

Shawn was held in jail over-night and appeared in juvenile court the following day. Since he was a teen-ager and a first offender, the judge gave him only four months in the reformatory, to be released on a year's parole in Irene's custody when she returned from her cruise.

Norma Davis, with two broken ribs in addition to her facial injuries, spent a month in hospital. She never really recovered from the beating and died a year later.

Is Anyone There?

Nathan Swartz was an impatient man and had always been so. He was born early; his mother said that; 'He wanted to get on with life.' As a small child he preferred toys with action—cars, trucks and trains—and grew very angry when they didn't perform as desired. In Grade School his sharp mind gave good results and his fine memory upset more than one teacher who contradicted herself. He had his Bar Mitzvah on the day that he turned thirteen in order to: 'Get it out of the way.' In High School rugby was his sport—all action. When World War II arrived, Nathan was 15 years old and afraid that the war would be over before he could get into it. At age 18 in 1943, having just finished High School, he joined the R.C.A.F. He wanted to be a pilot but his short stature (just 5'6") and his mathematical skills on aptitude tests led him to be a navigator. He arrived in England in mid-1944 and got in a tour of operations on Bomber Command before the war ended; he was awarded a D.F.C.

Returning to B.C. after the war (he had been born and raised in Nanaimo) he went to U.B.C. on his credits to study mathematics and accounting. Here he met a dark-haired beauty named Gloria Feinstein who was taking her B.A. in English. Nathan proposed almost at once and they were married in 1950, the day after he graduated. Gloria wanted to wait but Nathan said: 'Let's get at it.' He already had a job lined up with a firm of Chartered Accountants in Nanaimo.

They bought a large house because Nathan said: 'The kids will be along soon.'

'Not too soon,' Gloria remonstrated. 'I want to teach for a few years.'

It turned out to be only a few years because their first child (a boy) was born in 1953 and the second (also a boy) in 1955. Gloria did not return to teaching but did a lot of volunteer work when the boys were old enough. She had a calm, easy-going nature which nicely offset Nathan who was impatient, quick-tempered and iras- cible at times. Gloria calmed him down and stuck with him be- cause he was also loving, loyal, hard-working and a good provider.

Now it was 1994. Nathan had recently retired at age 70 but worked part-time at home. An expert on taxation, especially the hated G.S.T., he found no lack of clients in Nanaimo, the fastest growing city in Canada. Everybody had trouble with the G.S.T. which was full of exemptions, redundancies and ambiguities. McLean's Magazine called the G.S.T.: 'The most complex and ex- pensive tax regime in the world.'

If one bought any number of muffins up to five, one paid G.S.T.; if one bought six muffins—no G.S.T. A plain croissant was not taxable but if one added jam one added G.S.T. In one lecture that Nathan had attended, the expert needed 88 pages just to explain a single clause on drop shipments—goods imported with the help of a sales agent. Furthermore, Ottawa added and dropped G.S.T. at will and often with very little notice. Nathan had as much work as he wanted.

On this day, Gloria collected the mail from the box in front of the house. The family home was now too large for them with the boys gone but neither wanted to move. At age 70, with grey hair and rather poor teeth, she still had signs of her former beauty: clas- sic profile; thick, sensuous lips; dark, flashing eyes. She scanned the letters; one was from the Dept. of Veterans Affairs. She knew what it was and a wry smile crossed her lips as she remembered. Nathan's D.F.C. carried with it an honorarium of $50 a year. For many years after the war this arrived in December and was useful for Xmas. Then one day in the 1960s, Nathan almost had apoplexy when he received a cheque for $4.17.

'Look at this!' he shouted.

'Calm down,' Gloria demanded. 'What is it?'

'That stupid Government.' he fumed. 'Instead of sending $50 a year, they are now going to send me $4.17 a month.'

'How ridiculous.'

'Fancy them sending out hundreds, maybe thousands, of cheques every month for $4.17.'

'Oh, well,' Gloria mollified. 'You can't change it… remember that saying about things you can't change.'

'Stupid idiots,' Nathan grumbled, 'these little cheques will be more trouble than they're worth.' And they were.

Gloria chuckled at the remembrance. She put the mail on the hall table; none of it was important enough to disturb Nathan who was working in his den. Since his heart operation a few years ago, a three-way bypass, she had been very solicitous of his health and tried to avoid him getting upset. She went into the kitchen and started to prepare lunch but was distracted by a shout from the den: 'Gloria!'

Nathan's desk was a mass of papers. Hanging on the wall above was a faded wooden sign given to him by Gloria many years ago which read:

> 'PLEASE, GOD, GIVE ME PATIENCE.
> AND I WANT IT RIGHT AWAY!'

He was working on a problem for a large bakery in Nanaimo. It appeared that Corn Starch was subject to G.S.T. but exempt if it was used in bakery products. But the Act wasn't clear. Since the bakery used a lot of Corn Starch, a considerable amount of money was at issue. He decided to phone Revenue Canada in Victoria for clarification. He looked up the number and pushed the requisite buttons on his phone. Then he sat back in his chair, pushed one more button, and was stunned at the rapid-fire barrage of information that streamed over the line. He put the receiver down, took off his glasses, and shook his grey head as if to clear his brain. Then he shouted: 'Gloria!'

'She appeared in the doorway, 'Yes, dear?'

'Get a pencil and a piece of paper and pick up the extension phone in the kitchen. Try to write down everything you hear.'

'What is it?'

'It's a recording at Revenue Canada. I'll try to write it down as well… maybe between the two of us we'll be able to get it all.'

'All right,' she agreed. 'Give me a minute.'

Nathan phoned Revenue Canada again and they both scribbled furiously as a female voice rattled off instructions. Comparing notes afterwards, they agreed that the recording said:

> 'WELCOME TO OUR REVENUE CANADA

TELE-MESSAGE CENTRE. IF YOU WISH
SERVICE IN ENGLISH—PUSH BUTTON
ONE. IF IN FRENCH—PUSH BUTTON
TWO. (Nathan pushed One) THE
FOLLOWING SERVICES ARE AVAILABLE:
FOR GENERAL TAX INFORMATION—
PUSH THREE.
FOR CHILD TAX CREDITS—PUSH FOUR.
FOR CUSTOMS—PUSH FIVE.
FOR G.S.T.—PUSH SIX.
FOR A LIVE SERVICE REPRESENTATIVE—
PUSH SEVEN.'

'Amazing!' Gloria said.

'True,' Nathan agreed. 'Thanks for your help. I need some G.S.T. advice, so I'll call them.'

He pushed the buttons, ending with six for G.S.T.; he got a recording:

'I'M SORRY. ALL OUR LINES ARE BUSY AT
THIS TIME. PLEASE HOLD OR TRY
AGAIN LATER'.

Soft MUZAK flowed.

Nathan cursed and pushed button seven for a live person; the line disconnected. He slammed down the receiver and barely resisted the temptation to hurl the telephone across the room.

He started again, this time ending with seven in the hope of getting a live person to talk to. He heard the phone ring at the other end. 'Hooray!' he said. But no one answered. He let it ring ten times but still no answer. He swore again and hammered down the receiver.

By mid-afternoon, after numerous attempts, he had still failed to reach any number at Revenue Canada. Gloria brought him a cup of coffee. 'How's it going?' she asked.

'I give up,' Nathan replied, sadly. 'Either all the silly servants are busy with their gudgeons or there is nobody there. This return is due in a few days so I don't have time to write a letter. I'll just make my own interpretation and let it go.'

'It's absurd. The Government has gone mad with this voice-mail stuff.'

'They sure have,' he agreed. 'You can just see what will happen in the future. I'll have a heart attack and you won't be home. I'll push 911 and get a recording that says:

'IF YOU ARE USING A TOUCH
TELEPHONE—PRESS ONE.
IF POLICE ARE REQUIRED—PRESS TWO.
IF A FIRE IS IN PROGRESS—PRESS
THREE.
IF YOU ARE HAVING A HEART ATTACK—
PRESS FOUR—AND GIVE YOUR
MEDICAID NUMBER.
IF ALL LINES ARE BUSY—PLEASE HOLD.'

Gloria chuckled. 'You should call your Member of Parliament and complain.'

Their M.P. was of the Reform Party and Nathan had not voted for him. Still, an M.P. was supposed to look after all his constituents no matter what their affiliation.

'I'll just do that.'

Nathan looked up the number and pushed the requisite buttons. He got a recording:

'YOU HAVE REACHED THE OFFICE OF
JOHN MORTON, M.P. I'M SORRY—THE
OFFICE IS CLOSED TODAY. IF YOU WISH
TO LEAVE A MESSAGE PLEASE DO SO
AFTER THE TONE.'

After the tone, Nathan Swartz blew a large raspberry.

No sooner had Nathan put down the receiver when the phone rang.

'Is that Mr. Swartz?' a smooth male voice asked.

'Yes,' Nathan replied, warily.

'How are you today, Sir?'

'Frustrated,' Nathan growled.

'I'm calling on behalf of the Bird Watcher's Society on our campaign to save the Spotted Owl. Do you realize that this rare bird faces extinction because the Government is allowing forestry on those few areas where the Owl has its habitat. Now just a small donation would…'

The voice droned on and Nathan resisted the urge to use a few choice expletives. He hung up. 'Damn phone,' he grumbled, 'you can't live with it and you can't live without it.'

Old-Timer's Disease

Arthur Ingles leaned tiredly on his shovel and realised that he could not finish the job that he had set out to do. He wanted to plant a camellia bush in one corner of his yard but he could not dig any longer. A stroke one year ago had left him partially paralysed down his left side and with much less energy than he previously had. He sighed. He was a quiet, introspective man, 76 years old, resigned to his fate. His hair was sparse and grey; he wore glasses at all times and was a little hard of hearing.

Since he already bought the bush, he would have to ask his son, Howard, to come over and help him out. Standing there, looking at his house and garden, he knew that he could not take care of the property much longer. He sighed again; was a nursing home the next step? He shook his head sadly.

On the following day, a Saturday, he phoned Howard and explained the problem: '… and I can't dig the hole, the earth there is very hard.'

'I'll be right over,' Howard said. To his wife, Lorna, he shouted: 'I'm just going over to Dad's to help him with something.' He was a tall, vigorous man, 46 years old, with dark hair and eyes and a heavy beard.

'All right,' she replied. 'Will you be back for lunch?'

'No. I'll have a bite with Dad.'

'Okay.'

Their houses, in the Oak Bay district of Victoria, were not far apart. As he drove, Howard mulled over his father's situation. Obviously, he would soon have to give up the house. Howard disliked the thought of an old-folk's home. His house was large enough to take Arthur in, now that William was away in Vancouver at U.B.C. but he could not make such a commitment without talking to Lorna.

Howard dug the hole, planted the camellia bush, and helped his father with some other chores. They made a sandwich for lunch at which time Howard broached the subject of his father's future. 'Is this place getting too much for you now, Dad?'

'I guess it is,' Arthur replied. 'After your mother died, three years ago now, I thought it would be best to stay on here. Y'know… give me plenty to do so I wouldn't be too lonely. But now, after that stroke… and I can't drive any more… it's getting to be more than I can handle.'

'Is your neighbor still driving you around for shopping and all?'

'Yes. He even drove me out to Pat Bay for a reunion; he's a God-send.' Arthur had been a marine biologist at the Ocean Science Centre at Pat Bay. 'It's a burden to him, I know, but he never complains.'

'Yes,' Howard agreed. 'It's hard for either Lorna or me to help you much during the week since we both work.'

'I realise that.'

'In fact, I'd better be going now… I have to go into the office for a while this afternoon.' He was an economist and Assistant Deputy Minister of Finance for the Provincial Government.

'Even on a Saturday?'

'Yes… too much paper work.'

'Okay… thanks for coming over.'

'No sweat. We'll drop by tomorrow, too. In the afternoon.'

'That's great… 'bye.'

After dinner that evening, Howard spoke to his wife about his father: '… and he can't cope with the house and grounds any longer.'

'He has some help, doesn't he?'

'Just for the garden.'

'He could get some inside help, too.' Lorna took a comb to her hair; blond at one time, it was now a mousy colour but abundant. She was tall and well-proportioned; saved from being pretty by sharp features, small eyes and a pursed mouth. She was 44 years old.

'I suppose…' Howard started.

'Shouldn't he be in a nursing home?' Lorna interrupted. 'He might have another stroke at any time.'

'I don't like the idea of him in one of those places.'

'You don't know anything about them,' she said sharply. 'They are much better now than they used to be!'

Howard's face darkened. 'I know this, old people sent to a nursing home believe they are being sent there to die and they do. Dad needs some T.L.C. and is lonely without my mother. He won't get either of those fixed in a nursing home.'

'Well, we can't give him very much… we both work long hours.' She was a computer analyst with the University of Victoria.

'I think we should take him in,' Howard said, firmly.

'What?!' Lorna raised her eyebrows.

'Look,' he explained. 'That will bring him into our environment. We're home evenings and weekends. We've got a big, four-bedroom house and there is only the two of us. We could cut a door between the two bedrooms at the end of the hall. One could be a sitting room with his comfy chair, TV, VCR, books and whatever else he wants to bring. The bathroom is just outside the door and we have our own.'

'You've thought this all out, have you?'

'Yes, but I haven't said anything to Dad. I wanted to talk to you first.'

'I suppose we could.' She capitulated slowly. 'Bill will still have his room when he comes home.'

'So—do you agree?'

'I guess so.' Lorna was clearly not thrilled at the prospect. 'He's the only oldster we have.' Both of her parents had been killed in a car crash many years ago.

'Good! Thanks. I'm playing golf in the morning. Let's talk to Dad in the afternoon.'

Arthur Ingles, dreading the thought of a nursing home, quickly accepted his son's offer. They held a giant garage sale and disposed of everything that Arthur wanted no longer. His house, in a prime area of Victoria, sold immediately. In just over a month, Howard and Lorna had made the necessary changes and Arthur moved in.

Arthur was close to a perfect tenant. He was quiet, well-mannered and never raised his voice. He liked to read and wasn't averse to doing some work in the garden. His ex-neighbor still drove him to doctor's appointments and the like. He often took a bus to downtown. In the evening he usually stayed in his rooms. The only complaint that his son and daughter-in-law had was that Arthur's TV was rather loud; he was a little hard of hearing.

Nevertheless, Lorna's workload increased at once. Meals had to be made for three instead of two. She tried to get soft foods because Arthur, with limited use of his left hand now ate, he said: 'Like an American… fork only in the right hand.' Although he made his own lunch, she had to ensure that there was something to make it with. The laundry was larger. She left him to clean his own rooms but that didn't seem to include the bathroom so she did it. There was no telephone in Arthur's rooms so they had a jack installed; as well as a cable TV connection.

Lorna did not complain. After six months the routine in the household settled in place and Howard and Lorna were glad that they had taken Arthur in. They were soon to change their minds.

Lorna usually arrived home around five o'clock; her hours at the University were quite regular. Howard's hours were a bit erratic and he phoned if he was going to be later than six o'clock. On this day, Lorna stopped to do some shopping and got home at five-thirty. Placing the groceries on the kitchen counter, she saw that the tap in the sink was running. Cold water. She turned it off, shaking her head.

'Arthur… I'm home.' she called. She had been in some doubt as to what to call her father-in-law. She didn't want to call him 'Dad' because he wasn't her father. 'Art' sounded too familiar. So she settled for 'Arthur'.

He came into the kitchen. 'Hello.'

'Arthur,' she said, sternly. 'You left the tap on in the sink. It's a good thing the stopper wasn't in; the whole place would have been flooded.'

'I didn't leave it on.'

Lorna's eyebrows raised. 'Well, there wasn't anybody else here.'

'I don't care… it wasn't me!' he shouted. 'I wouldn't do a stupid thing like that! You're just saying that because you don't like me.' His face contorted with rage. 'You never wanted me here and I can leave any time I want to.' He stalked out of the room.

Lorna was stunned. This wasn't like Arthur at all. He was always calm and reasonable and never raised his voice.

In his room, Arthur put his head in his hands as he sat down.

Why had he turned on Lorna like that? She must be right... he must have left the tap on... there had been nobody else in the house. But he couldn't remember doing so.

When Howard came home Lorna explained what had happened: '... and he turned on me in a fury and said that I hated him.'

'That doesn't sound like Dad,' Howard soothed. 'I'll talk to him.'

But it wasn't necessary. When Arthur came down to dinner, he apologised to Lorna for his outburst.

'Don't worry, Dad,' Howard said. 'I've left a tap running before today, myself.'

It was the Ingles habit to take a small excursion on the weekend. It got them away from the house and made a treat for Arthur who could no longer drive. One Saturday evening Howard suggested: 'Let's take the ferry to Saltspring Island tomorrow... poke around the shops in Ganges... they have some nice Native stuff.'

'Good idea,' Lorna agreed.

'That would be nice,' Arthur added.

'Settled.' Howard got up from his chair. 'Would anyone like a drink?'

'I'll have a sherry,' Lorna said.

'Weak rye and water,' Arthur asked.

Howard mixed the drinks; a scotch and soda for himself.

After a few minutes of conversation, Arthur suddenly asked: 'What are we doing tomorrow? Are we going somewhere?'

Howard and Lorna exchanged looks. It had been only a few minutes ago that they had agreed to go to Saltspring Island. Howard explained it to Arthur again.

One day a week, Arthur took the bus into Victoria, had lunch and browsed around, particularly in Munro's Book Store. This day, when it was time to go home, he couldn't remember what bus to take. He started to ask someone but couldn't remember where it was that he wanted to go. He sat dejectedly on a bench. What was going on? What could he do now?

Daylight faded. Arthur still sat on the bench. At home, Lorna and Howard began to worry as seven o'clock approached. Where was Arthur?

Finally, a middle-aged lady noted Arthur's predicament and sat down beside him. 'Can I help you?' she asked, kindly.

'I don't know how to get home,' he replied, sadly.

'Where do you live?'

'Don't know.'

She put a hand on his arm. 'What is your name?'

'Can't remember.'

'Have you got a wallet?'

Arthur fished in his pocket. 'Yep… here.'

The lady saw that his name was Arthur Ingles. The only address that she could find was that of his previous house. 'Here we are… your name is Arthur Ingles and you live on Rosslyn Street, that's in Oak Bay. Shall I get you a taxi?'

'You're very kind,' he said, 'yes, please… a taxi would be fine.'

Arthur thanked her again when the taxi arrived. It took him to his old house. Suddenly, he remembered that he had moved to Howard's and how to get there. He directed the taxi driver.

Lorna and Howard were very relieved to see him. 'Where were you?' Howard asked. 'How come the taxi?'

'I met an old friend,' Arthur lied, 'and we got talking and forgot the time.'

'I don't see…' Howard started.

Lorna interrupted. 'I'll warm up your dinner,' she said to Arthur. Her silent communication of wide open eyes and raised eyebrows said to Howard: 'We'll discuss this later.'

Howard got the message.

After Arthur had gone upstairs to his room to watch TV, the Ingles discussed his plight. 'What do you think happened to him today?' Lorna asked.

'I don't know. I think he got lost and he didn't know where to go.'

'Then how did he get home in a taxi?'

'Maybe he met somebody who knew where he lived.'

Lorna snorted. 'That's very unlikely. Do you know if he has any identification on him?'

'I'm sure that something in his wallet will give his name and address.' Howard shook his head. 'I guess somebody helped him. His short-term memory is going fast.'

'Yes' she agreed. 'He often calls me Vera.'

'That was my mother's name.'

'I know.'

'Guess where I found his watch?'

'Where?'

'In the sugar bowl. And yesterday there were two pieces of burnt bread in the toaster.'

'Oh, hell!' Howard swore.

'And he always leaves the bathroom extractor fan on,' Lorna continued, 'because he can't hear it.'

'I'd better have a talk with his doctor,' Howard sighed.

'That's Dr. Packer, isn't it?'

'Yes.'

'Do you have time?'

'I'll make time.'

'Oh, dear,' Lorna sighed. 'Now I'll worry all day about what Arthur will get up to when we're not here.'

'So will I.'

Two days later Howard had a talk to Dr. Packer. As soon as they were alone, Lorna asked: 'What did he say?'

'He wants to see Dad... I made an appointment for next week. Meanwhile, I have to get a Medic-Alert bracelet for Dad in case he strays again.'

'Does he think it's Alzheimer's?' Lorna's voice faded. The dread word hung in the air between them like an atomic cloud.

'I'm afraid so.' Howard's head fell to his chest as he slumped in his chair.

Arthur Ingles looked at the bracelet on his wrist. He couldn't remember why he was wearing it but did remember that Howard said never to take it off. He looked at his watch. Three o'clock. He decided to walk into Oak Bay Village for a cup of coffee and look in the shops. As he passed the green sward of the Lawn Bowling Club a twinge of memory flashed; the place was familiar but he didn't remember that he had once bowled there.

In the village he saw a large sign in front of a shoe store that said 'SALE'. He went in and bought a pair of shoes that he didn't need. He wandered around for a long time. His legs grew tired as did his right arm from carrying the shoes. Spotting a restaurant, he went in for a cup of coffee. Over the coffee his mind went blank; he couldn't remember who he was or why he was there. In desperation, he kept ordering more and more coffee until the waitress became concerned and spoke to the manager: '... and he just sits there ordering more and more coffee. I think there's something wrong with him.'

'I'll call the police,' the manager said.

The Village of Oak Bay has its own small police force and a car was there within minutes. The policeman quickly saw the Medic-Alert bracelet with Arthur's telephone number and address. 'Come on, old fella,' he said. 'I'll drive you home.'

The police car and Lorna arrived home at the same time. The policeman explained the circumstances: '... and you'll have to keep a closer watch on the old chap.'

'Yes... thank you... we will,' Lorna said. To Arthur she said: 'Let's go into the house and make some dinner.'

'Yes, Vera,' he replied.

Howard took some time off work to take his father to the Doctor's. Howard worked plenty of unpaid overtime and was not concerned about taking a bit of time off during the day. Dr. Packer examined Arthur alone and then called Howard in for a talk.

Driving home, Arthur was silent for a long while and then turned to his son. 'I've got Old-Timers Disease, haven't I?'

'Alzheimer's. Yes, Dad... you have.'

'I'll have to go into a home, won't I?' Arthur's voice was so pathetic that Howard flinched.

'We'll see... we won't rush into anything.'

'I don't want to be a burden to you.'

'You're not,' Howard lied, wondering how much longer he and Lorna could cope.

For the next few weeks, Arthur did not leave the house and grounds. He seemed to sense that whenever he did there was trouble. But he was no longer the quiet, reserved gentleman that he had once been; he was now a querulous old man, sarcastic and impatient when things were not to his liking.

The climax came when Arthur decided to prepare dinner. Having spent three years living alone after Vera died, he was a competent cook. He was hungry and his watch showed the time to be 5:45 P.M. Both Howard and Lorna were late; there was no way that dinner could be had around six o'clock as usual. He would surprise them by getting the meal started. One of his favorite meals was fish and chips. He found some frozen fish in the refrigerator and some potatoes under the sink. He knew that Lorna had a chipping pan full of vegetable oil and found this in a cupboard. He turned on the oven to let it heat up for the fish. He cut up the potatoes and put the chipping pan on a high light to heat it up.

Then he had to go to the bathroom. He went upstairs and, after using the toilet, saw the TV through the open door to his sitting room. He decided to see if there was anything interesting on. He found a program on Muslim atrocities in Algeria that was fascinating. He forgot all about his dinner preparations.

When Lorna came home at six thirty, the burning oil had flowed over the stove, on to the floor and was in imminent danger of starting a fire. 'Good God!' she exclaimed. She turned off the burner and opened the front door to let the fumes out.

Just then Howard came home. 'What on earth...' he started.

Lorna shook her head. 'It looks as if Arthur started to make some chips, put the oil on a high light and then forgot all about it.'

'Good thing we came home when we did; the whole house could have been on fire. Where's Dad now?'

'Upstairs... can't you hear the TV?' Lorna replied, crossly.

Howard got some paper towels and began to clean up the mess, remarking: 'It looks like we'll need a new floor.'

The TV noise stopped and a few seconds later Arthur appeared. 'Oh, good, you're home,' he said. 'What's all that mess around the stove?'

'Don't you know?' Lorna asked, scathingly.

'Of course not.' Arthur replied, indignantly. 'I haven't been in the kitchen since lunch time.'

The Ingles looked at each other; it was pointless to pursue the matter. Lorna said to Howard: 'Do your best with this mess. I'll go and get some Kentucky Fried Chicken for dinner.'

'Oh, good,' Arthur said. 'That's one of my favorites.'

Later that evening, when they were alone, Lorna said: 'He'll have to be put away. He's too dangerous to be left alone now.'

Howard massaged his forehead. 'Yes… I guess so. I'll start to look for a place.'

'It can be one of the best homes. He has lots of money from the house sale. And he has his pensions.'

'I know but…'

She saw his distress. 'They'll take good care of him… make all his meals… he'll find friends there.'

'Yes.' Howard stroked one eye with a forefinger.

'And he'll be able to take most everything that he has here, so he'll have familiar things around him,' she continued, desperately. 'And you'll be able to visit him often.'

'Yes,' Howard said sadly. 'I'll be able to visit him but it won't be long before he doesn't know who I am.'

'It's not your fault, dear.' Lorna soothed.

'Then why do I feel so guilty? Why do I feel as if I've failed him? It was up to me after my mother died… I'm the only child… now look where I've led him.' Howard took out a handkerchief and blew his nose furiously.

Lorna blinked back tears as she put an arm around his shoulder: 'I'm sad and sorry, too.'

Dear Ann Landers

Heather O'Reilly (nee Andrews) looked at the mirror and sighed. She was fat. Her husband, Gordon, used such euphemisms as plump, well-endowed and said that he liked women with a bit of heft. But 30 pounds overweight was just too much. Her psychiatrist had it right—he referred to her as 'obese'. She thought that her round face, wide brown eyes and abundant brown hair with only a little grey at age 41 were all pleasant to look at. Her waist was not too large, even after two children. She often wore trousers to hide the varicose veins in her legs. She sighed again—she would have to find a diet that she could stick to.

Meanwhile, her sister, Tanis was coming for lunch and the house needed a bit of tidying. She had already made a salad.

Tanis Ellis (nee Andrews) rolled her car into the driveway, gave a brief tap at the front door and walked in. 'Hello,' she called, 'I'm here.'

'Hi,' Heather gave her a hug.

Tanis handed Heather a bag, 'Here's dessert… just some doughnuts.' Tanis, 45 years old, was slim and didn't have to watch her weight.

'Oh, you shouldn't have…' Heather said. 'How was the traffic today?'

'It's not too bad this time of day. Took me half an hour.'

'I wish we all lived nearer,' Heather said. 'You live in West Vancouver, me in Coquitlam, mother and Herbert in the city. It usually takes 45 minutes to go and see one another.' She bustled around, setting the table. 'How are Ken and the kids? Is Ken's business still good?'

'Yes, fine.'

Heather envied Tanis her opulent house provided by Ken's large income as an insurance broker.

'Do Keith and Warren come home for lunch?' Tanis asked.

'No... their High School is too far away.'

'Keith finishes this year, doesn't he?'

'Yes... he's eighteen. Warren has two years to go.'

'What will Keith do? Does he want to go to University?'

'No. Gordon wants him to take a mechanics course and come to work in the garage but Keith doesn't really want to. I don't know what he'll do.' Heather paused to inspect the table. 'There... come and have some lunch.'

As they sat down, Tanis asked: 'Have you heard from mother lately?'

Heather toyed with her salad. 'Oh, yes... she's stopped driving now... we have to go and get her for a visit.'

'Oh, hell!' Tanis swore. 'Twice as much driving for us. Did she have an accident?'

'I think she had a scrape. She was never a good driver... Dad did it all.'

'Well, he's been dead for over six months now. She should sell the car. I'd buy it and give it to Dan.' Her son, Daniel, was 19 years old.

'Why not give it to Janet... she's a year older than Dan.'

'Her boy friends all have cars.' Tanis said, sadly. 'They all drive so fast... I hope she isn't in an accident.'

'You worry too much,' Heather said. 'Do you still lock all the doors and windows when you're alone in the house?'

'You never know who is out there,' Tanis said, defensively. Worry lines creased her forehead and she wrung her hands together. 'Just read the paper about break-ins and rapes and everything.'

'You should see my psychiatrist.'

'Well... maybe,' Tanis refrained from saying that Heather's psychiatrist hadn't helped much with her weight problem. To change the subject, she asked: 'What about Herbert? Have you heard from him lately?' Herbert was their middle brother, between them at age 43.

'No. He seldom calls and every time I call him, he's drunk.'

'Oh, dear,' Tanis cried.

'Look,' Heather said. 'I'll have you all over for dinner next week—kids and all. I'll give Herbert plenty of notice, so maybe he'll be sober.'

'That should be good,' Tanis temporised.

From the front window, Heather watched her sister leave. 'What a screwed-up family', she thought. 'I'm fat... Tanis locks herself in the house and won't go out at night... Herbert is an alcoholic and probably homosexual... and mother is...' She couldn't find the right word.

Herbert Andrews mixed his fourth Scotch of the evening—or was it his fifth? No matter. He cursed himself for a fool for the umpteenth time for not thinking quickly enough when Heather phoned with her dinner invitation and pleading a prior engagement. Now he had not only to go but to pick up his mother since they both lived in the city. That was tomorrow. He dreaded the thought.

The feelings that Herbert had about his mother reminded him of the old definition of mixed feelings: 'Seeing your mother-in-law driver over a cliff in your new car.' He was sorry for her, now living alone since his father had died a few months ago. A debt of gratitude was there for the years of his youth and the financial help to see him through U.B.C. But her constant carping criticism and complaining drove him out of his mind. She never quit.

He sighed and mixed another drink. No work tomorrow—it was Saturday. Not that that made a lot of difference to his drinking habits. He knew that he was barely hanging on to a mundane government job and didn't care. He remembered the dull and degrading jobs that his sisters had taken just to get away from their mother's harassment—Tanis as a hair-dresser, Heather in a McDonalds. No wonder they both quit work when they married and never returned.

Herbert prepared for bed. He lived alone in a small apartment, shared occasionally with a member of either sex. He had not found a constant companion and wasn't worried about it. He took no exercise and his body was soft and flabby. Red veins on his cheeks testified to his excess drinking. His hair was dark but thinning. He would have trouble sleeping. Should he take a pill? He settled for another drink.

On the day of her family coming for dinner Heather bustled around, dusting and cleaning. When her father died, her mother,

Rose, had given Heather several large statuettes, vases and a wash-stand. These items, Rose said, were family heirlooms that were too big for the small suite that she had moved into and Heather could keep them in her house. But Heather thought that they were just junk and made her living room look like a second-hand store. So she put them away in a closet and took them out only when Rose came to visit.

Herbert pulled up in front of his mother's condo at exactly five o'clock, as arranged. Rose Andrews was waiting in the foyer. Entering the car, she said: 'Well, it's about time.'

He looked at his watch. 'I'm not late.'

'I didn't mean that,' she snapped. 'I mean it's over a month since anyone came to get me.'

'Oh… I'm sorry, mother.'

Rose sniffed the air. 'Have you been drinking?'

'Yes,' Herbert admitted. 'I've had a couple.'

'I know your COUPLE,' Rose said, sarcastically. 'No wonder you never get a promotion at work.'

Rose patted her grey hair, which she had just had coiffed, and adjusted the glasses on her nose. Apart from a touch of arthritis in her hands and feet, and a heart murmur, she was in good shape for her 70 years.

'Don't drive so fast.'

'Sorry,' Herbert slowed down.

'Watch that car on your right.'

'I see him.'

'Isn't it faster to take the Barnet Highway.'

'Perhaps,' he agreed, and turned left at the first opportunity.

And so it went. Herbert avoided any small talk for fear of retaliation. The car ride caused Rose's thoughts to drift back in time.

She recalled the family car trip from Alberta to B.C. in 1930; she was five years old and thrilled with the mountains. And they had to go through the United States to get to Vancouver! She had forgotten why they had to move. Perhaps the Church had made her father move; he was a Baptist minister. How she quaked in church—she had to go every Sunday—when her father threw down fire and brimstone like some wrathful Jehovah pouring vengeance on his deserving parishioners. She knew that the Devil would take her to Hell if she was bad. But it was so hard to be perfect.

She always had to be well-dressed, even through the depression when money was scarce. Her mother, cold and dour, said: 'You are not like the other children; you have to set an example.' How she wished that she had some brothers or sisters so that they could set an example. But, alas, she was an only, lonely child.

Well, she had escaped from the parental domination when she married Clifford Andrews. He was a good man but weak. It took all of her perseverance to turn him into something. And he would have spoiled the children had she not put her foot down. Still, she missed him now that he was gone. Of course, the children still needed guidance and it was now up to her alone.

Heather gave her brother a hug and her mother a peck on the cheek as they entered the house. 'How are you, mother?'

'I'm fine,' Rose examined her daughter. 'You should give that dress to Goodwill... it's too small for you now.'

'Yes, all right.' Heather sighed.

In the living room, Ken Ellis and Gordon O'Reilly stood up to welcome Rose; Tanis gave her mother a hug. 'Hi, Mum.'

Gordon took drink orders and went into the kitchen. He made Herbert's extra strong to compensate for what he knew was probably a hard car trip.

Rose looked around the living room and commented: 'I'm glad to see that you are taking care of the family heirlooms, Heather.'

'Yes, mother,' Heather replied.

Rose looked hard at Tanis. 'Did you mean to have your hair cut like THAT?'

'Is it too short?' Tanis' hair was cut in a Dutch Bob.

'Yes.' Rose snapped. 'It's not becoming someone your age.' She paused. 'Where are the children?'

'In the rec room,' Ken answered, 'playing a game.'

''Keith should be studying' Rose remarked 'considering his poor grades.'

'He'll graduate this year,' Gordon replied.

'But no honours?'

'No,' Heather admitted. 'He doesn't seem to want any further education.'

'He may come to work with me.' Gordon was a master mechanic in a Coquitlam garage.

'And Warren?' Rose persisted.

'He still has two years of High School left,' Gordon said. 'We'll see.'

Turning to Tanis, Rose asked, 'And what have you been doing lately?'

Tanis rubbed her hands together nervously. 'Not much. I've been collecting for the Heart Fund.'

'Good. Your father was always very generous to charities.'

Heather and Tanis looked at each other in amazement. Their father had been a child of the depression and very close with money; he almost never gave to charity. Heather raised her eyebrows at Tanis but said nothing.

Dinner was lively with the four young people talking. Warren, age 16, was enthusiastic about just obtaining his driver's licence.

'You be careful, now,' Rose admonished. 'Don't get into an accident.'

'I won't, Grandma.'

'Your Grandfather was such an excellent driver,' Rose said complacently.

Herbert choked on his wine. His father had been a very poor driver, continually berated by Rose both on and off the road.

Heather shook her head slightly and winked at Tanis. Their father had sure changed since his death.

As Gordon refilled the wine glasses, Rose said to Herbert: 'That's about enough for you... you have to drive me home, you know.'

'Yes, mother,' he replied.

'You, too, Tanis,' Rose continued. 'You know you have a low tolerance to alcohol.'

The lines in Tanis' forehead deepened, 'Yes, mother.'

Immediately after dinner, the young people disappeared. In the living room, Gordon offered liqueurs. Rose, Herbert and Tanis declined. Shortly afterwards, Rose said that she ready to go home. Herbert escorted her out of the house to the farewells of the others.

Heather and Tanis collapsed into chairs in the living room.

Heather said: 'Thank God, that's over.'

'I'll say,' Gordon agreed.

'Too right,' Ken echoed.

'Your turn next, Tanis,' Heather said with relief.

'It'll be a long while,' Tanis said wearily.

In fact, it was almost three months before Tanis summoned the courage to invite Rose and the family to dinner. It was not an enjoyable occasion.

Two weeks after that dinner Heather, Herbert and Tanis were startled to receive a letter from Rose. It said that, since their visits were now so infrequent, she would write a monthly newsletter about her activities and those of the family.

The first few letters were benign and innocuous. But then they changed to a litany of complaints: not enough visits; Herbert had missed her birthday; she had to spend a lot of money on taxis because there was no one to drive her; Keith still didn't have a job; Daniel had a speeding ticket; whenever she spoke on the phone to her grandchildren they showed little respect, and so on.

They all hated to receive Rose's newsletter. They didn't want to hear about their siblings troubles and they didn't want their own dirty linen exposed for all to see. Tanis, in particular, worried about the invasion of her children's privacy and feared that they would think this normal family behaviour. But what to do about it?

After a discussion with Heather, Tanis decided to write to Ann Landers and ask her advice. Tanis read Ann's column regularly and was impressed by her pertinent responses.

Tanis was surprised when her letter was published in the daily paper, along with Ann's reply, which read:

> 'WHAT I'M GOING TO SUGGEST WILL TAKE AN ENORMOUS AMOUNT OF SELF CONTROL. STOP READING THAT GARBAGE'

Tanis was stunned by the reply. How could she stop reading her mother's letters? True, they were obnoxious but they might contain something really important like Rose having to go into hospital or move to a nursing home or changing her will or her insurance.

NO! Ann Landers had blown it this time!

Lost Love

Louise Jones had been a very pretty child with curly blond hair, blue eyes, a dimple in each cheek and a peaches-and-cream complexion. People were always complementing her mother and patting Louise on the head. At age 16, in High School, she won a beauty contest in Vancouver and was selected to be Queen in the May Day parade.

All this attention had the result of her being vain, conceited and always very conscious of her looks. Louise had her choice of boy friends and chose the dark, brooding Arnold Hartnell who had a certain lusty sex appeal. They dated through High School and afterwards when she was working in a Supermart.

To the despair of his father, Wilfred, who was a university graduate, Arnold had neither the desire nor the aptitude for higher education. Since Arnold had a mechanical bent, always tinkering with cars, Wilfred found him a job as an apprentice to an engineer who worked with heavy equipment.

In 1998 Louise found that she was pregnant. She was 19 years old and Arnold was twenty. They married and a daughter, Donna, was born that same year. The marriage of the two young people never had much chance of success.

They rented an apartment on Clark Drive, not far from Arnold's place of work. There was no money for furniture; his parents helped them out with some from the family home and a forgiving loan for the rest. A car was out of the question. Arnold's job as an apprentice mechanic paid barely enough for them to live on.

From a care-free teen-ager, fond of parties and dancing, attuned to comments of her beauty, Louise went to a house-bound mother with a baby and no money for a sitter so that she could escape, even for a short time. Her own parents had been killed many years before in a car accident and she had been raised by an aunt whom she didn't much like.

Arnold would come home for dinner, give her a kiss, and ask: 'What's for dinner?'

'Bacon and eggs.' Louise was not much of a cook.

'Shit! That's breakfast stuff!'

'There's nothing else in the place,' she responded hotly. 'And I got no money.'

'Start it cooking... I'll wash up.' Arnold was a tall, dark man with bushy eyebrows, a lot of body hair, who always looked as if he needed a shave. He had a hair-trigger temper and looked threatening when he was angry. 'Where's Donna... asleep?'

'No,' Louise replied. 'She's in her play-pen in the bedroom. Bring her out with you.'

The bedroom was a mess—bed unmade and clothes scattered about. Arnold washed and picked up the baby, now a year old. 'How's my little sweetheart, eh?' He carried her into the kitchen. 'Christ! This place is a mess. What have you been doin' all day?'

'We went for a walk.' Louise turned the bacon over and added the eggs.

'You'd have time for a bit of housework if you didn't watch TV half the day and spend the other half in front of a mirror.'

Louise exploded. 'It's okay for you... out in the world. I'm stuck here all day with Donna and no money to go anywhere. If you earned a decent salary...'

The comment stung. 'I'll have my licence in another year and then I'll earn some dough.'

'Yeah... sure.' she scoffed. 'I don't suppose we could go out tonight—to a pub or a movie?'

'No, I'm broke. Maybe on Friday. We could get my mother to baby sit.'

Louise served the food. 'She doesn't like me.'

'Why do you say that?'

''Cause it's true.'

'They offen come to see Donna. She's their only grandchild.'

'Yeah... and every time they come your mother makes some remark about the place.'

'She's prob'ly right,' Arnold said, darkly.

Both Hartnell parents were disappointed in Arnold—their only child. Wilfred because he would not go to university and Beatrice because he had married so young and, in her opinion, beneath himself.

After taking a degree in Business Administration at U.B.C., Wilfred joined the Royal Bank and had worked there ever since. He was now a branch manager in West Vancouver where they lived. He was a quiet, soft-spoken man but forceful when he needed to be. An avid reader, he devoured several books a week and especially liked the biographies that Beatrice brought home for him. He was saddened by the fact that he had never seen a book in his son's apartment. Wilfred was 61 years of age and not looking forward to the bank's mandatory retirement age of sixty-five.

Beatrice, now 59 years old, worked in a branch of the Public Library in West Vancouver. After a variety of jobs in her early life, she quit working when Arnold was born and until he was of school age. Then she took a short librarian's course and had worked at that ever since. She was self-assured, tactful and a strong advocate of woman's rights. She didn't like her daughter-in-law but doted on Donna, her only grandchild.

Since both senior Hartnells worked, they usually only saw their son's family on the weekends. On this Saturday morning in 2000, they talked about the day's activities. 'Shall we try to take Donna out for the afternoon?' Wilfred asked.

'I'd like to,' Beatrice replied, 'but we'd better phone first. Louise doesn't like it when we just drop in. We probably catch her without her make-up on.'

'She's very pretty. She really doesn't need any make-up.'

'Yes. She's pretty... in a shallow sort of way.'

'You don't like her much, do you?' Wilfred raised his eyebrows. He was a tall man with grey hair and glasses who kept his weight under rigid control at a local health club.

'Not really,' she demurred. 'Donna is now two years old and Louise hasn't once invited us to come over. We always have to call them and they have only been here a few times.'

'True,'

'Of course, they don't have much money for frills but that doesn't matter.'

'They'll be better off when Arnold gets his mechanic's licence but he failed the exams this year so it will likely be next year before he gets it.'

'Does it make so much difference?'

'Yes… doubles his salary.'

'Oh. How about you calling them this time?'

'Okay.' Wilfred spoke to Arnold and it was arranged for them to pick up Donna at two o'clock.

When they knocked on their son's door, he answered. 'Hi… come on in.'

'Hello,' Wilfred responded. 'How's things? Louise not at home?'

'No. She went out to lunch with a girl friend.'

'Where's Donna?' Beatrice asked. 'In the bedroom?'

'Yeah,' Arnold said. 'You wanna put her outside things on?'

'All right.' Beatrice headed for the bedroom. She was neatly dressed in a tartan skirt and a plain brown jacket, every grey hair in place.

'We thought we'd take her for a car ride.'

'You gotta car seat for her?'

'Yes,' Wilfred replied. 'We bought one yesterday.' He paused. 'How are things at work?'

'Okay… we're fairly busy.'

'And at home?'

'Not bad. But Louise feels cooped up. Always bitching about something. Says she's gonna go back to work soon.'

Beatrice emerged from the bedroom with Donna dressed. 'Okay… let's go.'

With blond curly hair, china blue eyes and perfect features, Donna showed every promise of being as pretty as her mother. She clearly enjoyed the car ride and the Hartnells were entranced with her ready smile, gesticulations at the passing scene and adventurous attempts at new words. They both loved the child dearly and had to refrain from spoiling her too badly.

In the summer of 2001 Arnold passed his exams for a mechanic's licence and promptly found himself without a job; the company that he worked for had no opening for a full mechanic. He went on U.I.C. while he looked for work. Now money was even more scarce in the household and Louise's complaining evoked arguments which upset Donna who ran into her bedroom. After four months Arnold found a job.

'Where is it?' Louise asked.

'Up north,' he replied. 'On an oil rig north of Dawson Creek.'

'Where?!' She shouted. 'What the hell am I supposed to do while you're up there? I'll be stuck here with…'

Arnold raised his hand. 'Calm down. It's not that bad. Three weeks on and one week off… I'll fly back and forth. The pay is great.'

'Well, I'm not gonna sit around here and mope… I'm goin' back to work… Donna's old enough now for Day Care.'

'Look—it won't be so bad,' he soothed. 'I'll keep an eye open for a job in the city. This is just a temporary thing.'

'Oh, sure.' Louise was not convinced.

After Arnold departed for northern B.C., Louise returned to her job as cashier in a local supermart. Donna was put in Day Care. The separation put an end to the shaky marriage. Louise took up with a co-worker and Donna became accustomed to having an 'Uncle' stay overnight. Arnold heard about the affair and began to lie about his dates of coming and going in order to spend time with a previous girl friend.

The senior Hartnells watched the marriage dissolve with trepidation. They tried to take Donna for an excursion on every second week-end but it was not always possible. Secretly, they wished that they had her to raise but of course could not say so.

The divorce was bitter and acrimonious. Each accused the other of adultery. Louise was awarded alimony and custody of Donna. Arnold had visiting rights at those times he was in Vancouver. There was no property to split except for the tired furniture in the apartment which Arnold said Louise could: '…take it and shove it up your ass.'

Shortly afterwards, Wilfred phoned Louise on a Friday evening to arrange for taking Donna out over the week-end. He was surprised to find that an answering machine had been installed. He left a message asking Louise to return his call. To Beatrice he said: 'What do you make of that?'

'I don't like it.' Beatrice shook her head slightly.

'Do you think she'll call back?'

'I doubt it. She's never liked us much and with Arnold away…'

'If she doesn't call back,' he said firmly, 'we'll go over there in person next week.' He was a very deliberate man, not given to hasty decisions but quick to act once his mind was made up.

Louise did not return Wilfred's phone call. On the following Saturday, the Hartnells arrived at the apartment. Louise answered the door, holding it ajar and not inviting them in. 'Yes?'

'We'd like to take Donna out for a couple of hours,' Wilfred said.

'I dunno…' Louise started; although it was early afternoon, she wore an old housecoat and was disheveled with dark rings under her eyes.

'Did you have some other plans?' he asked.

Louise could not think fast enough to make some up and demurred: 'Well… I was gonna…'

Beatrice interjected firmly. 'Will you put on her outside things—or shall I?'

'I will.' Louise replied sulkily. 'Just wait there,' She closed the door.

The Hartnells took Donna for a car ride but there was a subtle difference in the child's behaviour. She shrank back a bit from Wilfred as he buckled her into the car seat. While she still enjoyed the passing scene, her comments were few and without her usual gesticulations. She didn't try any new words. When they returned to the apartment, she scuttled inside without her usual: 'Thank you, Grampa.'

The Hartnells sat in the car for a few minutes before driving away. 'What's going on?' Wilfred asked.

'I'm afraid to think about it,' Beatrice replied sadly.

The thought of being alienated from their precious grandchild filled them both with dread.

In the ensuing weeks they were unable to take Donna out. Louise always had a good excuse ready—doctor or dentist—or she was not at home. Then one Sunday, the Hartnells arrived to find the apartment empty—no curtains on the windows; a hollow knock. They found the caretaker, a wizened little Englishman of uncertain age with a face wrinkled like a prune. 'Yes?'

Wilfred explained who they were and '...do you know where Mrs. Hartnell went?'

'Calls herself Ms. Jones now, doesn't she?'

'Oh... well...'

'She's moved out, what?' he raised his grey eyebrows.

'I can see that,' Wilfred said testily. 'Did she leave a forwarding address?'

'No.'

'And you have no idea where she went?'

'No.'

'Did a moving company van come?'

'No... a Budget truck... with two young fellows, right?'

'Well... thanks for your help,' Wilfred said drily.

Driving home, Wilfred said: 'We'll have to find her.'

'Yes,' Beatrice agreed. 'We can't just abandon that child. Grandparents have some rights, too.'

'There's a detective agency that the bank sometimes uses. I'll get in touch with them.'

'Good idea.'

It took only two days for the agency to find Louise. Since she still had her job in the supermart, the detective simply followed her home. She had moved only a short distance to an apartment block very similar to the one she had just left.

The Hartnells then received a letter from Arnold saying that he was taking a new job at the Tar Sands Project near Fort McMurray in Alberta. He would not be in Vancouver very often and would they try to keep an eye on Donna.

But it was still proving impossible for them to do so. Although they now had Louise's new address and phone number, she always had some excuse as to why they could not take Donna out. Exasperated, Wilfred consulted his lawyer.

Mr. Barnes was a large, thoughtful man who listened intently as Wilfred explained the problem: '... so is there something we can do? Get a court order?'

Barnes stroked his chin. 'The B.C. Family Relations Act allows any person, related or not, to apply for access to, or custody of, a child. You seem to have excellent grounds for access, especially since the father has asked you to check on the child.'

'Will we have to go to court?'

'I'm afraid so. From the sounds of your ex-daughter-in-law, a court order will be necessary. The courts have stated that the best interests of the child must prevail and are very aware of the importance of the extended family. It should be no problem.'

Nor was it. Louise did not appear. The judge granted visiting rights of three hours every second week-end, telephone contact and the right to know about Donna's health and well-being.

When the Hartnells next arrived, on a Sunday, at Louise's apartment they were accompanied by a lady from Welfare with a court order. Louise had no choice but to allow Donna to go out with them.

But Donna was reluctant and Wilfred had to pick her up to buckle her into the car seat. 'What's the matter?' he asked. 'Don't you want to go for a ride?'

She looked downcast. 'My Mummy says you are bad.'

The Hartnells were shocked that Louise should so brainwash the child. 'But, Donna,' Beatrice chided tenderly, 'you know that's not true. You've been out with us lots of times.'

'You might take me away from my Mummy.' Donna gulped and a tear rolled down her cheek.

'Oh, dear,' Beatrice sighed. 'We would never do a thing like that.'

'No, never,' Wilfred agreed as he put the car in gear. 'Now you just look at all the interesting things as we drive along. And we'll stop for some ice cream.'

'It will soon be your fourth birthday,' Beatrice said, 'would you like to have a birthday party?'

'I'll have to ask my Mummy.'

Beatrice looked at Wilfred; she raised her eyebrows; the unspoken words were clear between them. It would take time, patience, tenderness and understanding to woo Donna back to them. But if love was the main criteria, they would succeed.

The Funeral Director

Richard Yancy became a Funeral Director more by accident than design. His father insisted that Richard go to university and learn a profession. But Richard was no scholar and one year of Accountancy at U.B.C. was all that he could stand. He quit and found a job in the tax department at Vancouver City Hall. It wasn't very satisfactory; the pay was poor, his boss was a woman whom he didn't like and since she was only a year or two older, promotion prospects looked bleak. Drinking beer with his cronies one night he complained loud and long about his poor situation. One of them remarked: 'Hey... with your long, sad face and smooth talk, you should be a Funeral Director.'

The idea appealed to Yancy. On enquiry, he found that there was a course for Funeral Directors and that two years of apprenticeship at a Funeral Home were required. He breezed through both and now, ten years later, was a Funeral Director at the Arbutus Funeral Home in Victoria. He drove a BMW, owned a posh condo on the harbour and, since he never married, women were plentiful.

On this day in 2002, he was sitting in his office waiting the arrival of Mrs. VanAllen whose husband had died yesterday morning. The Arbutus Funeral Home was the finest on Vancouver Island. It had a tasteful reception area, individual waiting rooms, two Chapels (small and large), a display room for caskets and urns, and underground parking. The staff were all certified and the Home was a member of the B.C. Funeral Association. It was also very expensive. It was Yancy's job to sell funerals at the highest price the market would bear. He was good at his job.

His intercom buzzed. 'Yes?'

'Mrs. VanAllen is in Endearment Room Number Two,' the receptionist intoned.

'I'll be right there.' Yancy picked up a file from his desk and paused to examine his image in a full-length mirror. His dark, three-piece suit was impeccable. He smoothed a bit of grey at one temple and straightened his tie which was a millimeter out of line. He composed his long, mournful face. Forty years old and not an ounce of surplus weight on his bony, 6'3" frame.

He was ready. He knew that Mr. VanAllen, now deceased, had been a noted city lawyer and quite wealthy. Yancy anticipated no financial hurdles in arranging an expensive funeral.

Entering the small but beautifully appointed waiting room he found Mrs. VanAllen standing. She was in her sixties wearing a black suit and a dark wig. Expensively dressed. Yancy took her hand; since he was so tall, he bowed towards her.

'I'm Richard Yancy, your Funeral Director. We spoke on the phone yesterday. Let me say again how devastated I was to hear of your husband's death.' This was somewhat of an exaggeration since Yancy had never met the man.

'Thank you,' She turned to a man in his forties with a round face and a soft, flabby body. 'This is my son, Andre.'

'How do you do.' They shook hands. Yancy moved behind the desk. 'Do sit down.' He opened his file. 'I think it would be best if we go through the form that we use; that way, we won't forget anything.' The form was three pages long. They went through the mundane family details and then Yancy asked: 'I believe you have a family plot?'

'Yes,' she replied, 'in Ross Bay Cemetery.'

'Good!' Yancy rubbed his hands together like an Arab bazaar merchant scenting a bargain. 'You will need a grave marker. We use Morton's Monumental Works; their granite work is superb. I happen to have a brochure of their's handy.' He passed a leaflet to the widow. 'Suppose you look this over and I get them to meet with us tomorrow?'

'That will be all right.'

'Fine!' Yancy didn't mention that granite was very expensive and that he got a kick-back from Mortons.

'I suggest that the funeral be held three days from now. Our embalmers do a great job; Mr. VanAllen will look quite natural.'

Andre spoke for the first time. 'Why does the body have to be embalmed?'

'For health and sanitations reason,' Yancy replied, 'as well as preservation of the remains.' He didn't add that embalming was not mandatory—they made a nice profit from it.

'Now,' Yancy continued, 'how many guests do you expect? Our large Chapel of Perpetual Peace seats about two hundred. Our smaller Chapel of Repose seats about fifty.'

Andre answered, 'About a hundred.'

'Then the large Chapel.' Yancy made a note. 'Your Minister is…?'

'Reverend Nelson of…' she started.

'Yes, yes,' Yancy interrupted. 'I know him well. I assume that you'll go over the Service with him… hymns, music, pictures to be taken and so on.'

'Yes.'

'Good. When that is all settled we will get the programs printed.' He paused. 'What about newspaper notices? Shall you do that or shall we?'

'I'll do it.' Mrs. VanAllen took a handkerchief from her handbag and dabbed at her eyes.

'It's a hard time, isn't it?' Yancy sympathized. 'Just a few more things. You will have to arrange for pall bearers. You may wish to place some personal things with your husband. Also, may I suggest a memory board with family pictures; if you like the idea, bring us the pictures and we will mount them.'

'I'll think about it,' Mrs. VanAllen said.

'Fine. Now… flowers. We use Cameron's Nursery… they are very good. Following the Service you may wish to present each member of the family with a flower from the Casket Spray.' Needless to say, Yancy got a kick-back from Cameron.

'Andre will see to the flowers,' the widow said, looking at her son, who nodded.

'All right… now a casket.' Yancy stood up, 'Shall we go along to our Containment Centre?' Yancy took her arm and led the way. Since he was so tall, he had to take short, mincing steps; he seemed to glide along. He was very pleased at the way things were going. No mention had been made of costs. With any luck he could get them to buy the new, solid copper casket (Price $5,000) that had just arrived. He would get a kick-back on that, too.

Thus Mr. Yancy's world was all in good order. Until he met Ronald Wittier.

Ronald Wittier and his wife, Agnes, retired to Victoria in 1999. They came from Saskatoon where they had both lived all of their lives. He had held a variety of jobs ending with work in a lumber-yard at his retirement. Wishing to escape the prairie winters, their choice of Victoria had been determined by their closest friends, the Allcots, who had come a year earlier. The Wittiers had never regret-ted their decision.

Ronald knew that he had an elderly aunt, Katherine Croft, in the area; she was his mother's sister and the sole survivor of that generation. He found her in the Victoria Nursing Home—age 95, in very poor health, with no other relatives in the area and very few friends. He began to visit her once a week, sometimes Agnes came along. They both felt sorry for the old lady who was so lonely. His Aunt Kay grew to depend on the visits and clearly appreciated their efforts. Both Wittiers often wondered how they would end up in later years. Ronald was 68 years old and had a heart condition; Agnes was 67 and had gall stones. Their only child, Eric, lived in Calgary. Their friends, the Allcots, were both older than they. Would the Wittiers be left bereft if they lived to Aunt Kay's age?

On the day that Yancy was fleecing Mrs. VanAllen, Ronald went alone to the Nursing Home with some freshly-baked cookies, cour-tesy of Agnes. He was startled to find the curtains drawn around his aunt's bed. A nurse was standing by. 'What is it?' he asked.

'She had a bad stroke,' the nurse replied. 'She is in a coma; the doctor doesn't expect her to live.'

'Oh, dear.' He was saddened by the news.

'The Administrator wants to see you.'

'Okay.'

'You know where his office is? By the front door?'

'Yeah.'

At the Office, a bald, rotund man named Blount, in his fifties, commiserated with Ronald and then said: 'Where do you want her body sent?'

'What?!' Ronald was stunned.

'I have her will here—we keep them on file. You are the Executor.'

'I am?' He had forgotten that his aunt had changed her will a year or so ago and had asked him to be Executor. 'Oh, yes… now I remember.'

'You also inherit… not that there will be much of an estate, I suppose.'

'Fancy that,' Ronald shook his head, his sparse grey hair.

'You should make arrangements with a Funeral Home,' Blount continued, 'to collect the body. Why don't you try the Arbutus Funeral Home… they are very good.' (He got a kick-back)

'All right. Did my aunt leave any money?' The Wittiers lived on pensions and had little spare cash.

'I don't know.' Blount stood up. 'Let's have a look through her papers.'

They discovered a bank book with a balance of $3,281.60. There was no sign of any other property. 'I guess that's it,' Blount said. 'Some of the furniture in the room is hers. We'll buy it from you if you like; we always have rooms to furnish.'

'All right,' Ronald said. To himself: 'Should be enough for her funeral, anyhow.' He was still stunned by the turn of events.

At home, he explained to Agnes what had happened: '… and she isn't expected to last very long.'

'That's too bad.' Agnes sat down heavily. She was putting a little weight on but her complexion was good and her eyes clear. 'I feel sorry for her. You don't know of any other relatives?'

'No, I don't. I've got her will here,' he held it up. 'I'd forgotten that I'd agreed to be Executor. I'd better read through it.' Which he did. 'Ah… it calls for her body to be cremated but it doesn't say what to do with the ashes.'

'What will you do?'

'Don't know. I have an appointment tomorrow at this Arbutus place. I'll ask them. I have to see a guy named Yancy.'

The moment that Ronald Wittier entered the Arbutus Funeral Home he felt uneasy and apprehensive. It was so opulent! His feet sank into the deep pile of the carpet. The furniture, some of it leather, was rich and expensive. The dark panelled walls had a deep sheen as if they were polished daily; they were graced with paintings—not prints, paintings. An elaborate chandelier hung from the ceiling. Exotic plants were placed in strategic locations. The receptionist—a candidate beauty queen—sat behind an antique desk.

At his enquiry, she led him to a small, tastefully furnished room with a plaque that read: Endearment Room Number Three. 'Mr. Yancy will be with you in a moment,' she smiled.

'All right,' he replied.

Yancy glided into the room. Since Wittier was only of medium height, Yancy towered over him. Introductions made, he said: 'Do sit down,' He moved behind the desk. 'Now… I gather that your mother is close to the end. These times are very difficult, aren't they?'

'It's not my mother… it's my aunt. The doctor doesn't expect her to live the day out.'

'I am here to serve you,' Yancy said, smoothly.

'Well, it will only be a small affair. My aunt out-lived her husband and her daughter… she's 95. So there's just me and Agnes… that's my wife… and a few friends from the Nursing Home.' Wittier paused. 'How expensive will this be?'

'It's hard to say until we settle all the details. We usually run to about 60 hours of work for a funeral. Plus material things, of course.'

'At how much an hour?'

Yancy squirmed; he was not used to such a question. 'It depends on how things are organized.'

Ronald did a quick mental sum. 'Let's see,' he mused to himself. 'Car mechanics now charge $70 an hour. This place won't be any less. Sixty hours at $70 an hour was $4,200. Hell! That was more than Aunt Kay had left by almost $1,000. Plus those 'material things'.'

Aloud, he said: 'My aunt's will says that she is to be cremated.'

'Fine,' Yancy replied. 'We are used to handling that.' He didn't say that he always tried hard to talk people out of cremation since there was less profit in it. Over 70% of people in B.C. were now cremated and the trend was rising.

'We have some lovely urns in our Containment Centre,' Yancy continued. 'It is usual to place the urn in a Memorial Hall, in a columbarium niche where it may be viewed through a protective glass behind a memorial plaque. This helps so much in overcoming grief.'

'How much does all this cost?' Wittier asked.

'Both urns and Memorial Halls vary a lot in price, depending on the customer's wishes.'

It was obvious to Wittier that he was never going to be able to pin Yancy down to any costs. It was also obvious that the Arbutus Funeral Home was far beyond his budget. Wittier was a child of the Great Depression and, while close with money, didn't mind paying a fair price for things but hated to be 'Taken'.

'We have a very nice, small Chapel,' Yancy continued, 'for your aunt's Service.' He opened a folder. 'Perhaps if we go through our standard form, we can get things organized.'

But Wittier was having none of that. 'Do you do the cremation here?'

'No, we don't.'

'Who does it?'

'We use the Oxford Crematorium.'

A thought struck Ronald. 'Why couldn't they pick up the body, do the job, and give me the ashes?'

Yancy's face grew even longer. 'Yes, that is possible but it seems a very casual way to treat a dearly departed loved one.'

'We could have a Service at the Nursing Home,' Ronald was on track now, 'they have a nice Chapel and that way her friends in the Home wouldn't have to go out. I could sprinkle her ashes in the sea. There's no law against that, is there?'

'No,' Yancy ruefully admitted. 'You could do it that way, but…'

'Then,' Wittier interrupted, 'we wouldn't need your services at all, would we?' He stood up. 'Thanks for your time, Mr. Yancy.' He marched out.

Yancy was stunned! He slumped back in his chair and shook his head sadly. He had never lost a customer like that before. That Wittier was sure a tough nut! Furthermore, he could have sworn that, although Wittier's right arm and hand hung straight down, the palm was turned up and the middle finger extended!

Arriving home, Ronald explained to Agnes what had happened:

'… and the Nursing Home will call the Crematorium when Aunt Kay dies and they'll collect her body. I have yet to contact the Minister for her Service but I have his name.'

'You've done good,' Agnes exulted. 'How much will it all cost now?'

'Under a $1,000, I reckon.'

'Great! And that Mr. Yancy was a real smoothie, was he?'

'He sure was,' Ronald replied. 'He reminded me of the story about the smooth, oily Funeral Director who was standing by the door after a funeral as the guests left. A very old, frail lady came tottering up on a cane. He rubbed his hands together and said: 'Hardly worth going home, Madam, is it?"

Addiction

Before I left for Brazil, I moved my mother into a nice Retirement Home in North Vancouver where I thought that she would be comfortable and safe. But it didn't work like that.

Just over a year ago my father died of a heart attack; it was unexpected because he had no history of heart trouble. But he was 85 years old and I guess these things happen. My sister Ruth, with husband and two sons, came from Calgary for the funeral but they couldn't stay. There are just the two of us, so it was left to me to sort things out.

At the same time my Company—a large mining outfit with world-wide interests—asked me to go to Brazil to fix some problems there; they thought it might take up to a year. I am their trouble-shooter. I agreed but requested a one-month delay in order to attend to my mother. This was granted.

The family home was a very modest house on Fraser Street in Vancouver. My father had been a desultory manual worker all his life and had never earned much money. (If I hadn't won a scholarship to U.B.C. I would never have got my engineering degree). But it sold quickly. I looked at several 'Homes' for my mother. Her health was poor—angina and rheumatism—and she was 82 years old. She was quite agreeable to the one I found in North Vancouver which had a resident nurse. The money from the sale of the house would pay her rent and see to her modest needs.

Thus I left for Brazil with a clear conscience. The job took ten months. The Chief Engineer was incompetent so I fired him and took over myself until I could find a replacement. The man that I found was a native who spoke the language; he had taken his degree at Queens University in Ontario and was familiar with our ways. When I left, I was satisfied that the mine would now be on a profitable basis.

I had left my Condo on False Creek empty; I didn't need the

money and wanted it available when I returned. After a day of getting settled and recovering from jet lag, I put in an appearance at the office and then went to see my mother.

'Hello, Mr. Evans… you're back.' The manager smiled at me from behind her desk in the lobby. She was slim, fortyish, immaculate and efficient, remembering me after almost a year.

'Yes, Mrs. Lindstrom… it's nice to be home.' I'd forgotten her name but there was a sign on her desk. 'How is my mother?'

'Emma is quite well.' There seemed a note of caution in her voice. 'She hasn't made any friends yet but she gets out regularly if the weather is reasonable.'

'Where does she go?'

'To the Park Royal Mall; it's just two blocks away.'

'She wrote that she had a new doctor. Is his office in the Mall?'

'I believe so.'

'Is she in her room now?'

'I think so; I haven't seen her down here.'

'Thanks… I'll go up.' I took the elevator to the fourth floor and knocked on the door. It took a full minute for her to answer.

'Hello, Mother.'

'Oh, Jason… you're here.' Her voice trembled.

'Yes.' I gave her a hug and looked closely. She had changed somehow. Her white hair straggled and her face was more lined, although her stocky frame seemed about the same. But her eyes were dull and, as we walked towards the living room, she shuffled along. She was dressed in a tartan skirt with a pale blue blouse but the buttons were fastened incorrectly and it bunched up in the middle.

'How do you like it here now?' I asked as we sat down.

'It's fine; they don't bother you.'

'Have you made any friends?' I knew the answer.

She looked vaguely around the room as if the question was too difficult to answer.

'Mother?'

'Oh, yes… I know the lady next door.'

'Is she nice?'

'What?'

'I said—is she a nice lady?'

'Who?'

'The lady next door.' I was at a loss to understand why she couldn't follow my conversation.

'Oh, yes.'

'What is your new doctor's name?'

'Visper or Vespir… like that.'

My mother isn't the smartest woman in the world but it's odd not to be sure of your doctor's name. (Neither she nor my father were intellectual giants and I often wondered where I got a Mensa I.Q. from). 'Do you like him?'

'Yes.'

'Is his office in the Park Royal Mall?'

'Where?' Her eyes roved the room.

'In the Mall down the street.'

'Oh, yes,' she replied, vaguely.

I couldn't figure out what was the matter; she seemed to be drugged. I tried again. 'Have you heard from Ruth lately?'

'Ruth?'

'You know… Ruth, Baxter and the boys.'

'Oh… yes… they are all well. They haven't been here since your father's funeral, you know.'

'They'll probably come soon,' I mollified.

'I don't suppose you'll get married now,' she said, sadly.

'I guess not.' I was approaching fifty and set in my ways. It wasn't that I didn't like women but just that I hadn't found the right one.

We chatted for a further half hour but it was very difficult for her to follow any train of thought; at one point she said that she had a headache. Before leaving, I went to use the bathroom. After washing my hands, I idly opened the medicine cupboard above the sink. I was stunned! It was full of medicine—bottles, jars, packages. Surely, she couldn't be taking all of this stuff?

I put on my glasses to read the fine print. I was started to find prescriptions from two different doctors—a Dr. Lanz and a Dr. Vospar. In addition, there was all sorts of patent medicines. I had my working clothes on and thus had a pen and a notebook in my jacket pocket. I wrote down the names of both doctors and what they had prescribed; the names of the drugs meant nothing to me but I would damn soon find out what they were! I also wrote down the names of some of the patent medicines.

I said nothing of this to my mother as we said our goodbyes. 'I'll see you in a day or so,' I remarked, giving her a kiss on the cheek.

She replied: 'That will be fine.' But there was no animation in her voice, no sparkle in her eyes; it was as if I were a stranger who happened at her door.

Driving home, I reviewed my options. There was no point in confronting my mother; she would just deny things, if indeed she was aware of exactly what she was taking. I was tempted to throw all the drugs out but of course some of them were needed. I wondered if I could get her into a hospital and have them sort her out. The first thing to do, I decided, was to talk to the two doctors who were prescribing for her.

At home, I poured myself a generous rye with a touch of water and looked in the Yellow Pages. I discovered that both Lanz and Vospar were Family Physicians and that both had offices in the Park Royal Mall.

On the following day I made appointments with both of them.

Dr. Lanz did not get up from behind his desk when I entered but waved me towards a chair. 'You wanted to see me about your mother—Emma Evans?'

I sat down. 'Yes.' He was in his sixties, tall (although sitting down), white hair, glasses and a large, fleshy face with red veins that denote a heavy drinker. 'How long has she been coming to you?'

He glanced at a file on his desk. 'About six months.'

'For what problems?'

He read: 'Rheumatism, lower back pain and headaches.'

'Did you know that she had angina?'

'No,' he replied, casually. 'She didn't say anything about that.' He looked at the file again. 'I took her blood pressure; it was a bit high but still within the normal range.'

'But you never listened to her heart or gave her an E.C.G.?'

'Yes and no. I listened to her heart and saw no reason for an E.C.G.'

I was very doubtful about that statement; if he had really listened to her heart, he would have known about the angina. I began to suspect that he was a pill dispenser of the worst kind. 'What did you prescribe for her?'

He read the file again: 'Ecotrin 10 for the rheumatism; Darvon for pain but that didn't seem to do much good, so then Dilaudid.'

'Did you tell her of the side effects of these drugs?'

'Don't remember; if she asked, I did.' He brightened momentarily. 'Have you seen these ads by an outfit called 'ASK'?'

'No.'

'They feature a prominent person—June Callwood is one—and advise Seniors to ask their doctor or pharmacist why they are taking this medicine and what the side effects are.'

'But you don't remember if my mother asked or if you told her?' I was getting disgusted.

'Nope... sorry.'

I decided not to tell Dr. Lanz that my mother was also going to another doctor. One way or the other, she would never come to this charlatan again. I stood up: 'Thanks for your time.'

'Anytime.' he waved me out.

Dr. Vospar's secretary/nurse said: 'The doctor will be available in a few minutes. Please have a seat.'

'Thanks,' I sat down.

She opened a file. 'You wish to see him about your mother... Mrs. Jason Evans?'

'Oh... oh,' I thought, 'she has used a different name.' Aloud, 'Yes.'

'Has something happened?'

'In a rather strange way... yes.'

Just then a patient emerged and I was escorted into the inner office. The nurse handed him my mother's file, saying: 'This is Mr. Evans.'

'Dr. Vospar.' We shook hands and he waved me to a chair while he scanned the file. He was in his forties, not very tall, dark hair, small goatee, piercing blue eyes. His three-piece suit almost disguised a small paunch.

'My nurse said that you wanted to see me urgently about your mother.' He had a slight mid-European accent; Czech or Austrian, I guessed.

'Yes,' I replied. 'May I ask how long you have been treating her?'

'About a year... ever since she moved to North Vancouver.'

'For what troubles?'

Vospar looked at the file. 'Primarily for angina and high blood pressure for which I am prescribing Vasotec and Nitrogard. She also has rheumatism and some lower back pain; for this she is taking Acetomin.'

I felt at ease with Dr. Vospar. 'Do you know that she is also getting prescriptions from another doctor... a doctor Lanz?'

'Oh, Lord!' His eyes widened and he half-rose from his chair. 'That can be very dangerous! Do you know which pharmacies she is using?'

'No, I didn't notice.'

'Has to be more than one,' he mused, 'because one would have spotted it. This Mall is divided into two parts and a shuttle bus runs between them. There is a pharmacy in each part... she probably used them both.'

'Probably,' I agreed.

'In a few months this won't be able to happen,' he continued. 'Are you aware of a program called PharmaNet?'

'No.'

'The B.C. Ministry of Health is going to make available to pharmacists computer access to people's medication profiles; the pharmacist will know at once if there is any drug conflict. The program was started because one in every four seniors admitted to hospital is suffering from a negative drug reaction.'

'Sounds great,' I responded, 'but it's too late for my mother.' I described the contents of her medicine cupboard and her strange, drugged behaviour: '... do you know this Dr. Lanz?'

'No. I know of him.' He didn't seem inclined to amplify the statement but his hooded blue eyes were hard. 'What is he prescribing?'

I checked my notes. 'Ecotrin 10 and Dilaudid.'

'Oh, dear.' He stroked his small beard. 'Dilaudid is very addictive and can cause severe headaches; it also reacts with other drugs.'

'Dr. Vospar,' I spoke firmly. 'I think the only way we can solve this problem is for you to come and see my mother.' He started to demur but I rode over his protest. 'If she comes to your office you'll never get a true story out of her. She won't say what drugs she is taking, if indeed she knows. Some of the patent medicines are very strong; one has codeine. Unless you cross-examine her in her own place where you can confront her with the contents of her cupboard and see for yourself just what she is taking, you'll not get her problem resolved.'

He grimaced. 'My schedule does not allow for house calls.'

'How about in the evening,' I persisted.

He raised his eyebrows. 'Possible...' He consulted his calendar. 'The only evening that I have free is tonight.'

'Nothing wrong with that,' I forced the issue. 'How about I meet you at her place at seven o'clock?'

He seemed a bit bemused. 'All right... seven o'clock.'

A few minutes after seven o'clock, I knocked at my mother's door. There was no answer. I knocked again. Still no answer. I tried the knob; the door was open. 'Mother?' I called as we walked in.

No reply. We walked through the living room into the bedroom. My mother was sprawled across the bed, fully dressed and unconscious. On the side table was an assortment of pill bottles. Her breathing was shallow and rapid. Dr. Vospar felt her pulse and pulled back an eyelid, muttering: 'Pupils constricted.' He opened his bag and turned to me: 'Call 911 for an ambulance... quickly!'

I ran to the phone in the living room. When I returned, Vospar was preparing a syringe. 'What is it? What are you giving her?'

'It looks like a drug over-dose. If we can get her stomach pumped out quickly she may be all right.' He felt for a vein and gave her an injection. 'This is just adrenaline to help her along.'

The ambulance arrived within minutes and the paramedics lifted her carefully on to a wheeled trolly.

'Put her on oxygen in the ambulance,' Vospar instructed, 'I'll follow you in my car.' They whisked towards the door.

'What hospital?' I shouted after them.

'Lion's Gate,' Vospar yelled in reply.

'I'll meet you there,' I shouted.

Before I left the suite, I found a garbage bag, emptied the contents of the medicine cupboard into it, and dumped it all down the garbage chute. Whatever happened now, it would be a fresh start as far as her drugs were concerned.

Down North

Joe Komiak sat in the small, wooden terminal building in Tuktoyaktuk waiting for the NWT (North West Transport) flight to Inuvik. It was over two hours late. Six other passengers, all Inuit, lounged around—equally bored. It was a day in mid-May, still winter in Tuk but a balmy -5° C and little snow.

The waiting room had a bench seat, a few chairs, a telephone and a faded map of the Territories on one wall. There were no windows. Not that there was anything to see, Joe mused, familiar to him as a native of Tuk it more resembled a moonscape than a landscape.

Flat and barren, no trees, rocky soil, the town of some 700 people sat perched on the shore of the Beaufort Sea. At one time it had thrived with the Hudson Bay Post and the DEW (Distant Early Warning) station. But both were gone now. The town was guarded by twin 'Pingos'. These mysterious little hills rose from the tundra like small, extinct volcanos but instead of flaming lava, their centres were blue ice.

Komiak's thoughts drifted ahead to his summer job, for which he was en route to Hay River. He was a Captain—the only Inuit Captain—of a tug which plied the Mackenzie River, owned by Horthland Transportation Company. It looked as if spring breakup would be early this year; he might be on the river by mid-June. He wondered about his crew changes; he would have a new Third Mate and five new crew men. Crew turnover was always high. Since NTC was unionized, all hiring was done in the Union Halls in Vancouver; he never knew who he was getting until they arrived. He was sad at the thought of leaving his family for the summer but this was the last time. He was 60 years old and looking forward to summers teaching his grandsons about Inuit customs and traditions.

The NWT aircraft finally arrived. The Twin Otter was the workhorse of the north, scarred and battered. Cargo was loaded at the front of the cabin, seats folded against the fuselage, with eight passenger seats in the rear. The co-pilot did all the work while the Captain sat in the aircraft with the starboard engine running. When all was loaded, the co-pilot shut the cabin door from the outside and entered by a crew door up front. The short flight to Inuvik was routine but it arrived too late for Komiak to make his connection to the south. He would have to stay in Inuvik overnight. He wasn't thrilled at the prospect.

By the time that Komiak checked into the Mackenzie Hotel and had a meal, it was early evening and the sun was still shining. He looked in the hotel bar, called the 'Zoo'; it was about half full of natives and whites but, since he didn't drink, he did not go in. Instead, he went out on to Mackenzie Road for a walk.

He knew Inuvik well and, although it was the 'Capital' of the far north, he didn't like the place. Four years at Samuel Hearne High School; after that, in the summer, Inuvik was usually the terminus for his barge train; in the winter he made regular trips from Tuk for supplies. He strolled along. It was a dirty town; beside the broken and intermittent boardwalk were cans, paper, bottles and other debris. A dog and a large Raven were scavaging. The buildings, all on pilings because of the permafrost, were shabby and unpainted. The ugly 'Utilidor'—raised metal pipe lined with fibre glass—ran through the town carrying steam heat, water and sewage. He walked to the end of the 'Utilidor', beyond which were unserviced native hovels and then turned around. Passing the Mad Trapper Bar, the walls of which are covered in signed, one dollar bills, the noise flowed out on to the street, along with drunken Indians. Komiak shook his head and hurried past.

The NWT B-727 took off at 0900 hours, bound for Edmonton with stops at Norman Wells and Hay River. Komiak got a window seat so that he could observe the Mackenzie River as they flew south. Between Inuvik and Fort Good Hope he could see open water in the middle of the river, a sure sign that break-up was on the way.

No single event in the north is as important as the spring break-up of the ice in the lakes, streams and rivers. Over the Territories flows a feeling of expectancy, a mood of euphoria, a relief that the long winter is finally over. The vast drainage area of the Mackenzie

River is larger than all of Europe and its life-giving tributaries the soul of its being. The river starts at Great Slave Lake which in turn is fed by the Hay, Slave and Athabasca rivers. During its 1800-Kilometre journey to the Beaufort Sea, the Mackenzie is replenished by such major rivers as the Liard, Great Bear and Peel. This huge arterial waterway is at once the commercial highway system of the north and the source of its communal life.

Cloud obscured the river about Normal Wells but clear skies over Great Slave Lake showed the lake to be open in the centre and only thin ice on the shore at Hay River. During the days when Hay River was a Hudson Bay post, the town was on low-lying, swampy ground and very susceptible to flooding. In 1963, after a great flood, the town site was moved several kilometres inland. The New Town is without distinction; hemmed in on three sides by heavy poplar forest and on the fourth by the Hay River, it is built in the form of a hollow square about two blocks per side. Around the square is the Ptarmigan Inn (with a flag pole bearing no flag and no visible means of raising one), the Silvertz Sports Center (small pool and large hockey rink), shops, Town Hall, two churches, school, and R.C.M.P. office.

Joe Komiak checked into the Ptarmigan Inn and immediately took a taxi to the docks to see his tug—the 'Marten'. Preparations for the coming season were underway. On the bridge, technicians were installing a satellite navigation receiver; they showed Komiak how it worked. Painters were busy on the exterior and in the crews' quarters carpenters were making changes.

He looked around with pride. It seemed a shame for this superb river vessel to bear the prosaic name of 'Tug'. Designed with a shallow draft of two metres especially for the Mackenzie River, the 700-ton boat was over 50 metres long and carried a crew of fifteen in relative comfort. Four 1125—horsepower engines gave it the power to push the heaviest train and side-thrusters the maneuverability needed for the tightest places. To penetrate darkness and bad weather the Marten had search lights that could illuminate eight kilometres ahead and dual marine radars that showed the smallest hazard to navigation. An echo sounder probed the river bottom; gyro compasses and direction finders plotted the course. Communications were more than ample: VHF to talk to other vessels and to shore stations, single-sideband to contact NTC at Hay River and walkie-talkies for the crew. The Mackenzie River tugs took second place to none.

The next few days were busy for Joe Komiak as he prepared for his first trip down river. He met his new crew members and got up-to-date with old ones; planned the timing of the Marten's route; determined the layout of the barges that would form his train. All of his barges were destined for Kilometre-136 of the new pipeline route, near the town of Fort Good Hope. They would not all arrive.

In 1977 the Berger Commission killed the Arctic Gas proposal for a pipeline from Edmonton to Inuvik, down the Mackenzie Valley. However, in 1980s a pipeline had been quietly built half-way down the Valley from Edmonton to the oil refinery at Norman Wells with hardly a word of protest from either the environmentalists or the Indian bands in the area. Now, after the discovery of massive oil fields under the Beaufort Sea, the government had given permission for the extension of this pipeline from Norman Wells to an artificial island in the Beaufort Sea. The only voice raised in protest was that of a group called the 'Native Organization for the Protection of the Environment'—abbreviated to NOPE. The acronym was generally taken to mean 'No Pipeline'.

NOPE had been formed by Susan Bavard, a young Louchoux Indian woman from Fort McPherson. She believed in pacifist demonstrations and had organized several in Edmonton and northern communities. But some of her followers—in particular Fred Tobac, a Louchoux from Fort Good Hope and the Alexi brothers, Robert and John, from Aklavik—scorned her policies and believed that only violence would achieve any results. Robert Alexi was one of Komiak's new deck hands.

Hay River was a funnel; into the cone poured the output of the C.N.R. line and the highway from Edmonton. Special rail cars had been designed to carry the massive 120-cm pipe and the heavy machinery for the pipeline. The dock area was jammed with the huge miscellania of items needed for the workers on the pipeline. The actual pipeline construction would be done in the winter when the ground was frozen to lessen environmental damage but all of the supplies had to be delivered in the short summer season that the Mackenzie was open.

On the tenth of June, Captain Komiak eased his barge train into Great Slave Lake. Directly in front of the tug was a new pipe-carrier barge with 500 tons of pipe; adjustable pushing bars on the tug fitted into the rear of the barge and a hydraulically-operated winch bound them together. Fixed to each side of the Marten was a 1500-Series barge and in front of each was another 1500-Series, fixed to the pipe-carrier. Thus the train was a coherent unit, pushed by the four powerful engines of the tug.

On deck, in charge, was Captain Komiak and his new Third Mate, Mike Murphy. The First Mate and the Second Mate and one engineer, although not on duty, were also on the bridge to watch the departure from Hay River. Murphy watched his captain closely; he had been skeptical when told that his captain was an Inuit. Of this there was no doubt; strong, stocky body; black eyes; swarthy complexion; iron grey hair. But Murphy, new to the river, was most impressed by Komiak's quiet orders and his deft handling of the large train, as he had earlier been impressed by Komiak's organization before departure.

As the train crossed Great Slave Lake, the onlookers left the bridge. Shifts were six hours ON/OFF and they would get some rest; although Komiak was always on the bridge for tricky parts of the river. He gestured to Mike Murphy: 'You take control... it's open water... get a feel for the train.'

'Thanks, Joe,' Murphy took the wheel. He was a tall man, 35 years old, with dark Irish looks and large hands and feet.

'Do a mild zig-zag,' Komiak ordered. 'That will give you an idea of how long it takes.'

Murphy did so. The pipe-carrier stretched for almost a city block in front of Marten. 'Jeez... takes time to turn, don't it?'

'Yes. We use the side-thrusters in narrow waters.'

Approaching the Mackenzie River estuary, Komiak took control again, although the river was 32 kilometres wide at the entrance. It would narrow to 10 kilometres at Beaver Lake and three kilometres at Fort Providence, where they would hit the first set of rapids. Since the Mackenzie flowed north, travelling down river was often referred to by the natives as going 'Down North'. The train made a speed of about 10 knots going down river.

It was quiet on the bridge, which Murphy didn't like. To make conversation, he asked: 'Is this your last summer on the river, Joe?'

'Yes. Forty seasons on the Mackenzie is enough for anyone.'

'Will you go back to Tuk?'

'Yes... that's my home,' he replied quietly. 'Where is yours?'

'Vancouver.'

'You have a lot of time on tugs?' Komiak asked; he knew the answer, having read Murphy's file.

'Yeah... but all ocean-going. This is my first time on a river.' He paused. 'Will we have to do a relay at the rapids past Fort Providence?'

'Maybe.' Joe replied. A relay meant taking the train apart and then pushing through one or two barges at a time. 'I'll wait until I see how high the river is there. This time of year, with everything in flood, it's often not necessary.'

It was warm on the bridge and they both shed clothes. Soon their shift was over and the First Mate, Emil Goodeve, and the Second Mate, Leo Hardy, took over.

Back on the bridge at the start of their next shift, Komiak took a look ahead with binoculars. He handed them to Murphy; 'You can see Fort Providence now.'

Murphy scanned the small town with its church spire and white frame houses. 'Who lives there?'

'Dogrib Indians,' Komiak replied, with the scorn of all Inuits for the Indians.

Murphy looked again. 'The houses, or at least some of them, seem to be raised up.'

'They are on stilts sunk through the permafrost.'

Murphy lowered the glasses. 'This is prob'ly a dumb question, Joe, but just what exactly is permafrost?'

'There are no dumb questions,' Komiak replied, seriously. 'Permafrost is a mixture of gravel, sand, peat and ice that is below freezing all the time. It's scattered down here but pretty well continuous north of Norman Wells.'

'How thick is it?'

'Anywhere from six to fifteen metres. Above the perma-frost is an active layer that thaws in the summer and freezes in the winter.'

'And how thick is it?'

'About a metre or so.'

'Thanks,' Murphy said. 'What about muskeg?'

'Oh, muskeg is just an Indian name for a swamp.'

At that moment the steady drone of the four engines changed in pitch. Komiak immediately looked at the rev counters; number one fluctuated, fell and then dropped to zero. The Marten slowed. The engine room phone buzzed. Komiak picked it up: 'Yes, Bob?'

The Chief Engineer, a wizened Scot of indeterminate age, was named Bob Carpenter. 'Joe, number one, port side, has failed.'

'I can see that,' Komiak said, drily, 'do you know what the problem is?'

'Not yet... give me a few minutes.'

'Okay... we'll struggle along on three.'

Fifteen minutes later, the phone buzzed again. 'Yes, Bob, what's the trouble?'

'Ah...' Carpenter hesitated. 'We'd better talk. Your cabin?'

'Two minutes,' Komiak turned to Mike Murphy. 'Take over... keep to the centre of the river.'

Murphy looked a bit startled. 'Yeah... okay.'

They arrived at the Captain's cabin at the same time. Komiak shut the door. 'What's up?'

'Sabotage.' Carpenter shook his head. 'That's what's up. Someone dumped sugar in the feed tank for that engine.'

Komiak's eyes grew hard. 'Do you know when?'

'Prob'ly at Hay River... there's not much security there.'

'Hell and Damnation!' These were Komiak's worse epithets. 'What will you do now?'

'I've isolated the tank; it will have to be drained and cleaned but we can leave that for now and by-pass it. But I'll have to strip the engine... the fuel injectors are all clogged... one fuel pump is shot...' His voice trailed off.

'We can run on three engines.'

'There's worse.' Carpenter shook his sparse, grey head. 'The port side-thrusters run off that engine... you can't go through the rapids without them.'

'Damn again! How long will it take you to get it running again?'

Carpenter rubbed a scratchy jaw between thumb and forefinger, neither very clean. 'Dunno... 12 to 15 hours, I reckon.'

'Well, get at it,' Komiak ordered. 'We'll lay up under Fort Providence until you're ready.'

'My boys are working on it now. What're you gonna tell the crew?'

Komiak sighed. 'Nothing. But there's probably no way to keep it a secret... likely all over the boat by now.'

'Yeah.' Carpenter ambled out.

Komiak got on the single-sideband radio to NTC at Hay River and told them about the engine failure but didn't give a reason; there was no need to tell the whole world.

The Marten lay stranded under the bluffs of Fort Providence whose total population, it seemed, watched from the cliff top and wondered why. The First Mate, Emil Goodeve, and the Second Mate, Leo Hardy, idled on the bridge with Komiak and Murphy.

'Whadda you think of the water height, Joe?' Emil asked. He was a robust man with a large paunch and a round bald spot on the middle of his head; he was 40 years old.

'I think it's high enough,' replied Komiak, looking at the nearby bank. 'We shouldn't need a relay.'

'Good,' Hardy commented. 'We're far enough behind schedule now.' Hardy was a Metis, slim and wiry, one of the few on the river.

Conversation was desultory. Mike Murphy lifted a cup of coffee to his mouth and spat out a bit of foreign matter. 'Pschoo... damn ice worm!'

'You shouldn't blame everything on the ice worm,' Komiak said, seriously. 'He is a friend of the Inuit.'

'Yeah?'

'Do you know his story?'

'No.' Murphy looked dubiously at his Captain.

'He comes from my village—Tuk. In the old days there was a kind and gentle Eskimo who loved all living things. One day he was buried in a snow-slide by an evil spirit who turned the snow into a wall of ice. The other Eskimos could not free him, the ice was too hard and thick.'

'And I suppose the ice worm got him out?' Murphy asked, suspiciously.

'Yes,' Komiak continued, without a trace of expression on his round face. 'Near Tuk, in a valley of happy things, lived the ice worm—Sikusi. He left his valley and went straight to the ice wall where he melted a path for the trapped Eskimo. The evil spirit left Tuk and never returned. So, you see, the ice worm is a sign of good fortune.'

'Yeah... well...' Murphy said, skeptically. Mythology was not his strong point. 'Just keep him the hell outa my coffee.'

The hours dragged by into the sunset; it would be followed by four hours of darkness. The motionless boat made the crew uneasy; like a bird with an injured wing. Komiak fretted but knew that no good purpose would be served by calling Bob Carpenter; he would be doing his best.

Making conversation, Goodeve said: 'Mike, what're you doin' up here—so far away from the salt-chuck?'

'I had a run-in with the union boss,' Murphy explained, 'thought I'd better get away for a while.'

'What kind of a run-in?'

'My boat went into drydock for a spell and he wanted me to take a shitty job up at Rupert. I wouldn't do it.'

'Did you have a fight?' Emil raised his heavy eyebrows.

'Yeah,' Murphy allowed. 'He kept buggin' me all night in the pub. Finally, I belted him one.'

'Were you drunk?'

'Not really... I had a few.'

'You Irish,' Goodeve laughed. 'Mike, do you know who the three most dangerous people in the world are?'

'No.' Murphy's eyes narrowed.

'A Jew with a law degree,' Emil continued, 'an Italian with an erection and an Irishman with a bottle of whisky.'

They all chuckled; even Murphy.

Komiak plugged in a cassette of 'Blackflies and Mosquitoes' which drove Goodeve and Murphy from the bridge, leaving the Inuit Captain and the Metis Second Mate to savour the songs that the WASPs didn't like. They listed to Bob Ruzicke:

> 'They built their towns and cities, built their
> hospitals and schools
> Brought their clocks, their calendars, their
> strange
> laws and their rules.
> People left their hunting trails and came in off
> the land
> To try and live a way of life they couldn't
> understand.
> Degraded by their welfare and destroyed by
> alcohol
> If you're not one or the other, you're not
> anything at all.

When darkness fell, Komiak went to get some sleep, leaving Leo Hardy in charge. At four o'clock in the morning Komiak was woken by Carpenter; the Marten was alive again.

Komiak wasn't sure whose shift it was but he wanted to handle the Fort Providence rapids himself. The water was high enough so that there was no chance of grounding but the eddys and swirls were dangerous to such a long train. He was glad that the pipe-carrier was low and thus he could see a long way ahead; he had had trains where the centre barge was stacked so high that visibility was restricted. Murphy watched in awe as his Captain picked his way through the white water like a dancing elephant in the circus.

After clearing the rapids, Komiak and Murphy turned the bridge over to Goodeve and Hardy and went for a meal and a rest. Soon the river spread out into Mills Lake, 20 kilometres across, which was famous for its sudden and violent storms but it was peaceful on this day. Goodeve remarked: 'Nice and quiet, eh?'

'Sure is,' Hardy agreed. 'Few blocks of ice still around, thought.' He pointed to the port side where a good-sized floe drifted.

'Yeah. You ever shoot ducks in this lake?'

'No, but I've hunted moose on the right bank ahead of us where the lake narrows. This is great trapping country, too. Beavers and rats in the spring, lynx and mink in the winter.'

The next sign of habitation was the small village of Jean Marie River. Only ten families lived in the pretty town, their log cabins standing bravely at the water's edge. North of the town, the countryside became more interesting; the river banks were more wooded and small islands dotted the Mackenzie, making Goodeve pay close attention to his navigation as he threaded the long train through.

Soon the Marten and her train were stopped at Fort Simpson. At the junction of the Laird and the Mackenzie Rivers, the town had spilled over from its original site on an island on to the west bank of the Mackenzie. A thriving town of some 2,000 people, it was the centre of activity for a large area of the Mackenzie valley.

Joe Komiak called Bob Carpenter and Emil Goodeve to his cabin. 'We've got two 600-Series barges of machinery to collect here. We'll put one in front on each side of the pipe-carrier and fixed to the 1500-Series behind. There's still enough daylight to do that. We'll stay here over-night and leave at daybreak. Any comments?'

'Yeah,' Carpenter said, 'what about the sabotage of my engine?'

'I was coming to that,' Komiak replied. 'I asked you both to keep an eye open for a suspect in the crew. Any ideas?'

'No,' Carpenter answered. 'I don't think it's one of the engine room guys... they all have too much respect for machinery.'

'It might be one of the deck hands,' Goodeve replied, 'but if it is, I don't know which one it might be.'

'Well,' Komiak said, 'we'd better post a watch all the time we are here.'

'Right,' Emil said, 'both inside the boat and on the train.'

'You organize it, Emil,' Komiak ordered. 'Two-hour watches.'

'Okay.'

After securing the two new barges, the crew of the Marten, except for those on watch, went into town. Most of them went to the Sub-Arctic Inn to have a drink and to meet old friends and acquaintances. Komiak, who didn't drink, went to the coffee shop at the Fort Simpson Hotel, another meeting place. Here he met an old friend, Father LaLonde, who had once been the Roman Catholic priest at Tuk.

'It's good to see you again, Father,' Komiak said, as they shook hands.

'Likewise, Joe.' The priest put his arm around the Inuit's shoulder. 'Let's have a coffee.'

'What are you doing here?' Komiak asked.

'Attending a seminar on alcoholic problems. I'm now waiting for a NWT flight back to Fort Good Hope.' Father LaLonde had a pinched, narrow face with weary, red-rimmed eyes and shoulders hunched as if he personally bore the weight of all the sins in the Territories.

'The perpetual northern problem, eh? Drink?'

'Yes,' LaLonde agreed. 'It's hard on the families, especially the children.'

'Was that story true,' Komiak asked, 'about the Indians from Good Hope hiring an aircraft at Norman Wells and filling it full of booze after getting paid off by Hire North?' His disdain for Indians was clear in his voice.

'Yes,' the priest sighed. 'They had been two months on the seismic lines and had much money. All I could think of was the clothing and food that could have been bought for the children. I'm afraid it has become a status symbol to bring in liquor in large amounts.'

While Komiak and LaLonde discussed the reasons for native drinking, Robert Alexi, the Marten crew man, nursed a beer in the Sub-Arctic Inn while waiting for the second-in-command of NOPE to arrive. He saw Fred Tobac heading for the table—a slight Loucheux Indian with ferrety features, restless black eyes and a pointed chin with a small scar. They exchanged high fives and ordered more beer.

'How's it goin', man?' Tobac asked.

'So far so good.' Alexi replied. 'We hit them pretty good at Fort Providence with that sugar in the gas tank.'

'Yeah… you done a good job there.'

'Does Susan Bavard know about it?' Alexi asked, referring to the head of NOPE.

'No… and she ain't goin' to.' Tobac paused. 'They're addin' two more barges here, ain't they?'

'Yeah… 600-Series with machinery.'

'I guess they'll be put in front?'

'They're already there… alongside the pipe carrier.'

'I hear that the Willowlake River is in full flood this year… lotsa logs and debris where she hits the Mackenzie.' Tobac rubbed the scar on his chin. 'Sure be a shame if them two barges got loose.'

'All hell would happen.' Alexi gave a thin smile. He was a heavy-set man with hard eyes.

'How are they fastened?'

'Two steel cables to the pipe carrier and the 1500-Series behind.'

'I got a battery-operated cutter.' Tobac's lips formed a cruel smile.

'And I got the midnight to two o'clock watch on the train,' Alexi exulted. 'Come along about one o'clock.'

'Will they hear the noise?'

'Nah… they'll all be asleep and it's a long way to the fronta the train.'

'Right on!' Tobac shouted for some more beer. 'Waiter…'

At day-break Emil Goodeve eased the Marten and her train out of Fort Simpson. Leo Hardy reported their departure to NTC by single-sideband radio. The high water of the Laird River gave them an impetus until he turned the train north on the Mackenzie. 'It's calmer now,' he remarked.

'Yeah,' Hardy agreed. 'But they say that the Willowlake is bad this year.'

'I hear that, too. Well… we'll see… or, rather, Joe will see.' Komiak had arranged the shifts so that he took over just before the Willowlake was reached.

'You ever been up the Nahanni Valley, Leo?'

'No. I hear it's pretty spectacular. The Virginia Falls are higher than Niagara. There's a place called Hole-in-the-Wall Lake where the water is 38° C.'

'What about that Headless Valley, where people go missing and then their heads are found later?'

'Ah, that's just a rumour,' the Metis replied. 'I think…'

As they proceeded down river, the rising smudge of the Mackenzie Mountains became visible. Soon six hours had passed. As Komiak and Murphy came on the bridge, Emil said: 'Joe, there's the crooked peak that marks the Willowlake River… about 10 kilometres ahead.'

'Thanks, Emil,' Komiak replied. 'Everything okay?'

'Yep… have fun,' Goodeve said as he and Leo Hardy left the bridge.

As the Marten neared the junction of the Willowlake Komiak could see that the river was indeed at full flood. The banks were stripped far above the high water mark. The churning water was a muddy brown colour with logs and debris swirling in the eddy currents. He eased the train into the turbulence and winced as a large log struck the port 600-Series barge. He was not worried; the train was built to withstand much rougher water. He didn't know that the steel cables on both 600-Series barges were only threads.

Another log and a pile of debris hammered the port side and then, suddenly, a vicious vortex caught the train and slewed it around. Some of the weakened cables on the starboard 600-Series barge parted with a 'Twang' that could be heard clearly on the bridge.

'Holy Mother!' Murphy whispered.

The train swayed ominously. Then all of the cables on the starboard barge parted and it broke away, floundering towards the east bank of the Mackenzie. Komiak fought the unbalanced train in the turbulent water, the starboard side-thrusters at maximum. Then the port 600-Series barge, its rear cables parted, careened into the pipe carrier. A Caterpillar tractor on the barge rolled into a row of pipes on the carrier and carried the lot into the water on the starboard.

Komiak doubted his senses as he fought for calmer water. The port barge then broke clear and headed for the east bank. Then a second row of pipe, whose retaining bars had been damaged by the first stack breaking away, rolled majestically into the river, sending up geysers of water.

There was a stunned silence on the bridge as the Marten cleared the turbulence into calmer water. Komiak guided the train to a stop near the small village of Camsell Bend, where several Indians had been watching the debacle. He organized work parties for the recovery of the two errant barges. 'Hell and Damnation', he swore. He still couldn't believe it; a Cat and 100 tons of pipe at the bottom of the river. What had happened? He had been through the Sans Sault Rapids when they were much rougher than this water today but had never had a barge break away. He worked like an automaton. Was he just unlucky? Was it the 'Jesus Factor'—an event over which one has no control? Was his last summer on the river to be a disaster? His shoulders slumped and his grey head dropped to his chest in despair.

He heard Mike Murphy call from one of the barges that they were winching back from the beach. 'Joe... hey Joe!'

Komiak left the bridge and walked down to the starboard railing. He could see Murphy holding up a piece of frayed steel cable.

'Jesus, Mary and Joseph!' Murphy yelled. 'It's been cut almost all the way through... they all have!'

Komiak's head came up, his shoulders straightened, his black eyes threw sparks, and his lips tightened his face into a fierce, dark scowl. 'So it's a fight they want! Hell and Damnation... they're gonna get one!'

•

The End

Author's Note: From the novel 'The Land God Forgot'

ISBN 141202282-7